Family Business

Servant of God

Book VI

Family Business Series

Family Business VI

Servant of God

Vanessa
Miller

Book VI
Family Business Series

Other Books by Vanessa Miller

Family Business Book I
Family Business II - Sword of Division
Family Business III - Love And Honor
Family Business IV - The Children
Family Business V - The Atonement
Family Business VI - Servant of God
The Spirit of Christmas
Sunshine And Rain
Rain in the Promised Land
After the Rain
How Sweet The Sound
Heirs of Rebellion
Heaven Sent
Feels Like Heaven
Heaven on Earth
The Best of All
Better for Us
Her Good Thing
Long Time Coming
A Promise of Forever Love
A Love for Tomorrow
Yesterday's Promise
Forgotten
Forgiven
Forsaken
Rain for Christmas (Novella)

Through the Storm
Rain Storm
Latter Rain
Abundant Rain
Former Rain

Anthologies (Editor)
Keeping the Faith
Have A Little Faith
This Far by Faith

EBOOKS
Love Isn't Enough
A Mighty Love
The Blessed One (Blessed and Highly Favored series)
The Wild One (Blessed and Highly Favored Series)
The Preacher's Choice (Blessed and Highly Favored Series)
The Politician's Wife (Blessed and Highly Favored Series)
The Playboy's Redemption (Blessed and Highly Favored Series)
Tears Fall at Night (Praise Him Anyhow Series)
Joy Comes in the Morning (Praise Him Anyhow Series)
A Forever Kind of Love (Praise Him Anyhow Series)
Ramsey's Praise (Praise Him Anyhow Series)
Escape to Love (Praise Him Anyhow Series)
Praise For Christmas (Praise Him Anyhow Series)
His Love Walk (Praise Him Anyhow Series)
Could This Be Love (Praise Him Anyhow Series)
Song of Praise (Praise Him Anyhow Series)

Prologue

Whether in the body or out of the body, Obadiah Damerae Shepherd did not know. But as he stood looking heavenward he saw a door open in heaven, and the first voice which he heard was like a trumpet, saying, "Come up here and I will show you things which must come to pass." And immediately he was in the spirit: and, behold, a throne was set in heaven, and One sat on the throne.

And He that sat was to look upon like a jasper and a sardine stone: and there was a rainbow round about the throne, in sight like unto an emerald. Round about the throne were four and twenty seats: and upon the seats, he saw four and twenty elders sitting, clothed in white raiment; and they had on their head crowns of gold.

Out of the throne proceeded thundering, lightning, and voices: and there were seven lamps of fire burning before the throne, which are the seven Spirits of God. And before the throne, there was a sea of glass like unto crystal: and in the midst of the throne, and round about the throne, were four beasts full of eyes before and behind.

The first beast was like a lion, and the second beast like a calf and the third beast had a face as a man, and the fourth beast was like a flying eagle. Each of the four beasts had six wings about him, and they were full of eyes within: and they rest not day nor night, saying, holy, holy, holy, Lord God Almighty, which was, and is, and is to come. Those beasts gave glory, honor, and thanks to Him, that sat on the throne, who liveth for ever and ever.

The four and twenty elders fell down before Him that sat on the throne, and worship Him that liveth for ever and ever, and cast their crowns before the throne, saying, thou art worthy, O Lord, to receive glory and honor and power: for thou hast created all things, and for thy pleasure they are and were created.

Then the angel said to me, "Come, I have something to show you."

Dam was then transported to another area where he saw another mighty angel come down from heaven, clothed with a cloud: and a rainbow was upon his head, and his face was as it were the sun, and his feet as pillars of fire. He had in his hand a little book that was open: and he set his right foot upon the sea, and his left foot on the earth as he cried with a loud voice, as when a lion roars: and when he had cried, seven thunders uttered their voices.

The angel which Dam saw stand upon the sea and upon the earth lifted up his hand to heaven and swore by Him that liveth for ever and ever; who created heaven and the things that are therein, the earth and the things that are therein, and the sea and the things which are therein; that there should be time no longer.

"What does he mean?" Dam asked the angel, "What don't we have time for anymore?"

The angel did not answer his question, but rather said, "God has called you to prophesy before many people, nations, tongues, and leaders. Be instant in season, for the time is short."

If this was what God wanted from him, then Dam was ready and willing. He just prayed that the love of his life, the woman he was set to marry in the morning was ready and willing also.

~~~

Amarrea Harris stood in front of the full-length mirror and exhaled. All morning long, through hair, make-up and as she put on her gown, everyone kept telling her how beautiful she was, but it wasn't until this very moment as the veil was being placed on her head and she gazed at the strapless white mermaid cut gown that she truly felt beautiful. It was such a special feeling. The lace and tulle had a royal effect that made her look and feel like a princess. No, not just a princess, but a much-beloved princess. At that moment, Amarrea knew exactly how Meghan Markle must have felt as she walked down the aisle in the Windsor Castle to marry Prince Harry.

She too was about to marry a prince. But this one didn't have a grandmother who was the queen of a nation. But Dam Shepherd did have a heavenly Father who was King of kings and Lord of lords. She twirled as she continued to look at herself and fantasize about the wedding she'd dreamed about all her life. Amarrea heard sniffles behind her. "None of that. This is a happy occasion."

Wiping her face with the well-used tissue, Amarrea's mom cleared her throat and said, "I'm just so happy for you, honey. Dam is such a good man, I know that he will treat you like a queen."

"And I know she will treat Dam like a king and that's why I can't stop crying either," Angel Shepherd, Dam's mother said as she reached out and lovingly adjusted Amarrea's veil.

"Okay, let's break this up. I don't need the bride crying and getting her makeup all messed up." Marissa Walker grabbed Amarrea's hand and pulled her away from the doting mothers. "Girl, you've got ten minutes before you walk down the aisle, think happy thoughts. We don't want the make-up artist to redo that mascara and eyeliner now, do we?"

Since the day they met in college, Marissa had become the calming force in Amarrea's chaotic life. They were destined to be best friends for life; Amarrea was glad that Marissa was her maid of honor. "Girl, if you weren't here I would have lost my whole mind instead of just pieces of it."

There was a knock at the door, the ladies watched as the door slowly opened. Isaac Walker Jr., Marissa's husband, peeked his head in the door. "I'm just following orders, ladies." He set his eyes on his wife. "The groom is in place. I'm going to take a seat now, okay?"

"Thank you, baby." Marissa walked over to the door and kissed her husband. "You're the best look-out man God ever created."

"You're just saying that because your birthday is coming up and you want that necklace, you slyly pointed out the other day."

Giggling, Marissa admitted, "Did you see how many diamonds that were on that necklace? Of course, I want it. But you're still the best man God ever created."

"Um, excuse me, but do you two lovebirds mind moving out of the way so I can get down the aisle and marry the real best man God ever created?"

The room erupted in laughter, but not for long because the moment Amarrea started walking down the aisle tears of joy flowed from the onlookers. Her prince was waiting for her. They loved each other, and she couldn't wait to spend the rest of her life with him.

1

Dam's heart filled with sorrow at the realization that he had missed God's direction when he accepted the youth pastor position at the church he currently worked for. He knew that God called him to evangelism… to prophesy to nations, but he took this assignment because Bishop Daniel Thomas persuaded him to believe that becoming youth pastor at his church was a part of God's plan for his life.

Dam had much respect for Bishop Thomas because he had been watching his world-renowned ministry on television for most of his life. The church was Called of God International Ministry, and they were on the mission field in Africa, Mexico, and India.

Bishop Thomas told him that although the ministry was flourishing, the youth ministry had fallen off because of a scandal their previous youth minister had gotten into. The bishop believed in the call that was on Dam's life and believed that he was the right person to rebuild the youth ministry. Dam told Bishop Thomas that God's call on his life was more of an evangelical/prophetic one. He believed he was supposed to go out into the world and preach the gospel. But Dam still didn't have a clear picture on how all of that was supposed to happen.

Bishop Thomas promised Dam that he would be able to evangelize the world by being a part of Called of God International

Ministry because he would be able to go on the mission field and preach the gospel to people in other countries, some, who have never heard the gospel.

Dam had bought the sales pitch and signed on to work for Bishop Thomas. The first year was actually one of the best years he'd had thus far in ministry. Dam and Amarrea bonded with the youth in the church and built that ministry from two hundred kids to a thousand. But that's when the problems started.

Dam was informed that he would not be able to go on the mission trips because they didn't have anyone to take over for him in the youth ministry. Dam didn't like it, but he stayed behind and did the job he had been hired to do. Then one Sunday while Bishop Thomas was in Africa doing missions the media department made the mistake of submitting Dam's sermon to the youth for the Sunday broadcast that was viewed by a little over five hundred thousand people.

Dam didn't think anything of it when it happened the first time, but the following Sunday the media department uploaded his next sermon to the television ministry, even though the viewership went up to a million on that broadcast, Dam wasn't pleased. Somebody was doing this behind Bishop Thomas' back, and he intended to get to the bottom of the matter.

However, before Dam could meet with the media department, Bishop Thomas called and accused him of trying to take over the ministry. "I didn't submit my sermon to the media department, Bishop. As a matter-of-fact, I scheduled an appointment with Vickie to figure out why my sermons were uploaded to your television broadcast."

"Vickie, who?"

Called of God International Ministry had over fifteen thousand members so Dam could understand that Bishop wouldn't know who all the workers in each ministry were. Vickie Gray had not only worked in the media department, but she was also a front door greeter and had served as armor bearer for Lady Jade, Bishop's wife. Vickie also sat in the quarterly minister meeting that Bishop held. "You know Minister Vicki Gray, sir. She's on our ministry team and armor bearer for your wife."

Bishop Thomas harrumphed. "Vicki knows better than to do some mess like that. I'll take care of her."

"Don't be too hard on her, Bishop. Minister Vicki has a lot on her plate. It might just be an honest mistake."

"Look here boy, you might be smelling yourself because the viewers loved your sermons. But I run Called of God and neither you or Vicki are going to take it away from me. The devil and all his imps done lied if you think rising up against me is a good idea."

Something in the way Bishop spoke to him that day made him want to turn in his resignation and pack up his office. But he and Amarrea had only been married sixteen months at the time and had been in the middle of purchasing their first house. He needed a steady income, so he stayed.

A year later Amarrea was now pregnant with their first child, and Bishop Thomas was on his way to Dam's office for another one of his little chats. Dam didn't know how much more he could take, but he also didn't think being homeless with a wife and a kid was a part of God's plan for his life.

The knock came like the police banging on a drug dealer's door, just before they broke down the door. The door swung open, Bishop stepped into Dam's office like he was evicting a deadbeat who had the nerve to ask for thirty more days on the premises. What had he done to offend the bishop today? Lately, it seemed like the very air Dam breathed offended his boss.

Bishop plopped himself in the chair that was seated in front of Dam's desk and proceeded to put his feet on the desk. Every single time Bishop did this, Dam felt disrespected, like Bishop was sending a message that Dam was beneath him.

"What in the world am I going to do with you?" Bishop leaned back in his seat as he kept a laser focus on Dam.

A look of confusion danced across Dam's face. "Sir?"

Bishop's feet came off the desk as he firmly planted them on the floor and leaned forward. "Don't give me that 'sir' crap. I have put up with your innocent act long enough. But I'm not letting you get away with this one."

"What are you talking about, Bishop? What have I done?"

"Two things I can't stand… a backstabber and a sneak. Turns out, you are both."

There were times when Dam wondered if this world-renowned pastor whose sermons were aired on three different television networks and two radio stations might actually be bipolar. Dam stood. "My wife is waiting for me. I need to get home."

"I wouldn't care if the Pope was waiting for you. I'm not finished with you. If you think I'm going to let you stab me in the back with Pastor Walker and keep your job here, then you need to think again." Bishop was in his face, practically foaming at the mouth. Spitting as he talked.

"You're upset about the revival I'm working on with Pastor Walker? But I told you about it two years ago."

"Yeah," Bishop admitted. "But I thought it was at least five years off or if it would happen at all. How could you and Pastor Walker pull something like this off without my help? You must have gone behind my back and used some of my contacts."

"We didn't use any of your contacts, sir. I have never gone behind your back for anything. Now if you'll excuse me." Dam tried to walk around him, but Bishop grabbed hold of his arm.

"Cancel the revival, or you can turn in your resignation."

"What?"

"You heard me. Maybe you should go home and ask your pregnant wife if she prefers having a roof over her head and food in her belly, or does she want you to do this revival that your boss and spiritual leader has instructed you to cancel."

When Dam didn't reply, Bishop patted him on the back, like you'd do an obedient dog. "I'm sure you'll make the right decision for your family."

Dam was too stunned to speak. He watched Bishop walk out of his office wanting desperately to turn in his notice on the spot, but Bishop Thomas was right. He needed to talk to Amarrea first.

~~~

"This is not necessary, Dr. Nance. I feel fine," Amarrea Shepherd said as she sat on the examination table.

"Your feet are swollen, and your blood pressure is up. Whether you like it or not, I'm taking you off work for the last three months of your pregnancy."

"You don't understand. My husband is a youth pastor. He doesn't make a whole lot of money, and we just bought a house. We need both incomes."

"You need to be healthy and to deliver a healthy baby. Believe me Amarrea I do understand. When I was in residency, my husband was serving as a missionary. Money was tight for us for many years.

But we made it through. This is a setback, but you and Dam will find another way to take care of the mortgage for a few months."

Amarrea looked down at her feet and admitted to herself that they were not only swollen, but they hurt. If she killed herself before having this baby, then her child would be without a mother and Dam would be without a wife. She sighed. "We'll make due. Dam wouldn't want me to continue working with my health at risk."

2

Dam had been introduced to Isaac Walker Jr. at his wedding a few years back. It turned out that Amarrea and Isaac's wife, Marissa were best friends since college. Dam had been fascinated by the stories Isaac told of the street revivals he used to do with his father. One thing led to another, and they began planning street revivals of their own. Dam was honored that Isaac thought enough of him to want to do street revivals with him. Because he was well aware that Isaac started doing street revivals as a teenager with his father, the original OG. Isaac Walker Sr. was a legend on the streets. Dam's grandfather, Don Shepherd, was a legend in his own right, but even he told stories about Isaac's dad.

Isaac Walker Sr. had made millions as a drug dealer who murdered anyone who got in his way. But after going to prison, he came out a changed man. Isaac Walker Sr. gave his life to God and set out to make right the wrongs he had committed. He brought many women and men to Christ and even began doing street revivals and brought even more people to Christ from those. After he passed, his eldest son Donavan Walker became senior pastor of the church and his youngest son, Isaac Walker Jr. became an elder at the church and was supposed to take over the street revivals.

For years, one thing after another kept getting in the way of Isaac's street revivals. He was finally ready to get back to his first love and believed that God had hooked he and Dam up for such a time as this. Now Dam sat in his car trying to figure the best way to tell his wife that he would have to quit his job in order to do what he believed God has as his next assignment.

Money was tight for he and Amarrea, and they needed both of their paychecks just to make the mortgage and put food on the table. But if they gave up eating out, stopped buying organic produce and cut off cable, maybe they'd be able to make it on Amarrea's income while he looked for another job. Amarrea wouldn't be off work until 11 pm, so he picked up dinner and headed home.

But when he pulled into the driveway and saw Amarrea's car, he immediately got a sick feeling in the pit of his stomach. Amarrea was a workaholic. She had not missed one day of work since he met her.

Rushing into the house, he shouted for his wife. "Amarrea… Amarrea."

"I'm in the bedroom," she yelled back.

Dam climbed the stairs two at a time. Dam put the bag of Chinese food on the bed next to Amarrea, noting that she had her feet propped on two pillows. "Your feet bothering you again?"

"It's worse than that."

Dam sat on the bed and put a hand on his wife's bulging belly. "This little one has been given you problems, huh? Must be a boy with a big head."

Amarrea hugged her stomach. "If it is a boy, he doesn't have a big head. He's perfect."

"Don't defend him. I know he'll have a big head because he's getting it from me."

"Well let's just hope if it's a girl, she doesn't inherit the big head Shepherd gene."

Dam leaned down and planted a kiss on Amarrea's lips. "You don't have to worry about that. If it's a girl, she is going to inherit her looks from you."

"And I pray that she inherits your heart for God from you."

They sat there gazing into each other's eyes. Taking in the moment. Because they both realized how special it was for the two of them to have met and fallen in love. Many people thought that the concept of a soul mate was not reality. But Dam knew better. Amarrea wasn't supposed to be working the ER the night his brother almost died. But the nurse on duty got sick and had to leave. They called three other nurses but only connected with Amarrea.

God made sure that Amarrea was in the right place at the right time so he could find his soul mate. The woman was the love of his life, and he would do anything to put a smile on her face. But right now, she didn't appear to be smiling. "What happened today, hon? You seem a bit down."

"I did get some bad news at the doctor's office today." She hesitated and then continued. "It appears that my feet are swelling because my blood pressure is up, the doctor has put me on bed rest until the baby is born."

His antennas went up. "What does this mean? Are you at risk for losing the baby? Are you okay?"

Amarrea put a hand on Dam's arm. "Don't get upset, bae. If I take it easy and eat the right foods, my blood pressure should come down, and the baby and I will be just fine. I'm just worried about you. I talked you into buying this house, and now I don't know how we're going to pay for it."

Dam's mouth dropped, but he quickly picked it back up. No way could he tell his wife that Bishop threatened to fire him today. Not with her blood pressure up and her worrying about how the bills will get covered. "We both love our home, and if I have to work two jobs to cover these bills, you are going to lay yourself in this bed and not worry about one single thing."

"But you can't work two jobs. Don't forget you and Isaac are preparing for the revivals."

He put a finger to her mouth. "You are not too worry about anything, that's an order. Do you hear me, Mrs. Shepherd?"

"Yes, but…"

He tapped his finger to her lip again while shaking his head. "Have faith in God and your husband. We got this."

Amarrea let out a sigh of relief and then laid her head back against her pillow. "One thing that should help. Since I'm going to be home, I won't be eating out all the time. That should save some money."

"See, we're already working this out. And I'll see if I can work from home one or two days a week to help you." Dam got off the bed. "Are you hungry? Do you want some of this Chinese food?"

"No, to the Chinese food. But I'd kill for a bowl of butter pecan ice cream right now."

"I thought you need to eat better?"

"Pecans are good for you and ice cream is really just frozen milk," Amarrea reasoned.

"I'm going to let you have that one today. I'll get your ice cream, but after today if you want something sweet, it's going to be fruit."

She saluted him. "Yes, sir."

He couldn't help but smile as he left the room. But he was serious about making sure that Amarrea watched what she ate. High blood pressure was nothing to play with. Unfortunately, Dam also knew that he couldn't just quit his job and cause Amarrea to worry about the bills. He checked the freezer to make sure they still had the ice cream, then he called Isaac.

This was going to be one of the hardest calls he ever had to make. Dam truly believed that the street revivals was God's next mission for him. But maybe God was saying not now. Isaac picked up on the third ring.

"You must have radar or something. I was just about to call you," Isaac said joyfully. "You wouldn't believe how many doors God has opened for us. I just received back to back calls from two networks wanting to broadcast at the revival. This thing is not just going viral, we are going nationwide, my friend."

Dam smiled, truly happy that things were going well with the planning of the revival. Even if he couldn't be a part of it, he wanted nothing but success for Isaac. Because if Isaac succeeded, that meant many souls would be saved. "I'm happy for you, man. But I've got some bad news."

"What's going on?"

"Amarrea is having complications with the pregnancy, she's been put on bedrest." Dam didn't want to tell the rest of it but thought he owed it to Isaac to be completely honest. "And Bishop confronted me today. He said that if I did the revivals with you, then he would fire me. I was prepared to walk away from my job... but I wasn't prepared for what Amarrea laid on me when I got home. I can't put any further stress on her right now and losing my job would definitely stress her out."

"No, you shouldn't stress out your pregnant wife, but I need you on my team. I know I heard from God on this. So, give me a few days to figure something out. Okay?"

Dam thought he'd heard from God also, which was why the thought of not being a part of the revival was an agonizing one for him. But he couldn't let Amarrea down. He would hold onto his job at the church and get a second job if need be.

3

Isaac was at his brother's house when he received the call from Dam. He walked to the kitchen to share his good news. But when Dam gave him the news he didn't want to hear, Isaac sat down at the kitchen counter and lowered his head. What in the world was he going to do now?

As he was running options through his head, his three-year-old son came barreling through the kitchen on one of his cousin's skateboards and knocked over a bowl of fruit Diane, his brother's wife, had on the table.

Isaac got out of his chair. He angrily pointed at his son, who lay sprawled on the floor. "Boy, what is wrong with you? Are you trying to tear down this house the same way you tear mine down?"

"Whoa, stop yelling at him. Donny told him to get on that skateboard. He took off before I could stop him." Marissa picked the fruit up off the floor and checked on Isaac the third, affectionately called, Junior.

"Why weren't you watching him? Why would you let that boy race through here like that?" Isaac knew he was over the top with his anger, but he couldn't stop himself. Nothing seemed to be going the way he wanted it lately.

Marissa gave Isaac a look that said, 'you know I'm not speaking to you the rest of the night, right?' Then she walked out of the kitchen without answering either of his questions.

"Bro, calm down," Donovan said as he came into the room. "Today is not the day you should be yelling at your family, especially since we both know you're not upset about Junior spilling fruit on the floor."

Isaac sat back down. Donovan was right. He had been depressed all day. The only bright spot had been when he received calls from those television producers. But even that hadn't changed the fact that today was his father's birthday. This was the reason he was visiting with Donovan. His half-sister Iona and her husband Johnny were there also.

This was supposed to be a celebration of their father's life, something they had done every year since the old man had been gone. But Isaac wasn't in the mood and hadn't been since his father died.

Donovan put a hand on his brother's back. "I've been praying for you. I know this is a hard day for you."

Shaking his head, Isaac admitted, "When I hear you and Iona laughing about things dad did when y'all were younger, it makes me angry because y'all had more time with him and mama than I did. I just wish they would've had me earlier."

"You can blame Donovan for that," Iona said as she entered the kitchen.

"Shut up, sis," Donovan playfully shoved Iona, trying to get her out of the kitchen.

"I'm serious, Donovan." Iona being her normal feisty self-was not going to let it go. Pointing toward Isaac, she said, "He thinks Mama-Nina and Daddy were more concerned with their careers than they were with having another child. He thinks they had him late in life because they didn't want any more children. Don't you think we owe him the truth?"

"Was there another reason that mama was in her fifties when she gave birth to me?" Isaac looked at his big brother with questioning eyes.

Nodding, Donovan said, "I guess our know-it-all sister is right. I got into some trouble when I was younger. A thug came after me. He wanted to kill me, but instead of shooting me, mama got shot. The doctors told her that she would never be able to conceive another child. And for many years that doctor was right. But then God blessed them with you. And they were overjoyed."

"Thanks for telling me that, bro. I knew that they loved me. But I grew up feeling like I was some oops kind of accident. I still wish I had more time with them. But I need to find a way to appreciate the time I did spend with them."

"Exactly," Iona said. "I don't like seeing you mopping around so much, little brother. And you've got to know that daddy and Mama-Nina wouldn't want you mourning for them so long."

"They wouldn't want me neglecting the revivals either. But I haven't done one since dad has been gone. That's been over three years."

"I thought you were taking care of that. I just gave my secretary the approval to pay the invoice for the massive field you rented for the revival."

"I've run into some problems," was all Isaac said.

"You need to talk to Keith. He and dad handled those revivals for years. You might be able to do a little brainstorming with him," Iona told him.

Donovan cocked his head to the side as he looked at his sister. "You know, for a big-mouth, you come up with some really good ideas."

Why didn't he think of that himself? Isaac had been spinning his wheels for years over this revival. Isaac reached over and hugged his sister. "You do have good ideas, sis. Thanks."

~~~

"Hey, Unc, how ya' be?" Isaac said as he sat down in the rocking chair on Keith Williams' front porch. There were two rocking chairs on the porch, just like the chairs his mother and father claimed they wanted to put on their porch as they went into retirement. Sadly, Isaac Sr.

and Nina went home to glory before they could get a chance to chill out on their porch. "I don't believe you actually put rocking chairs on your porch."

"I never imagined I could miss any human being this much," Keith said. "But when I sit out here on the porch, rock back and forth in this chair, I sometimes imagine that your dad is sitting right where you are, and we are chucking it up about the good 'ol days." Keith took out his handkerchief and wiped his eyes.

"I miss the old man too. I've been trying to get the street revivals you and he used to do back on track, and I've run into one roadblock after the next. I finally thought I was pulling it together. But I just received some terrible news."

"And you came over here hoping that I could fix your problem for you?" Keith chuckled as he kept rocking back and forth.

"I need to brainstorm Unc. I know that God showed me that this young minister Dam Shepherd was supposed to partner with me on these revivals. There's something that's in him, that God is going to use mightily. I don't know what it is, but God wants him. And Dam believes that this is the ministry God has for him as well."

"Okay, so what's the problem."

"I've got the locations secured. I was even able to get a Christian television network to film the revivals."

"That's something your dad and I never accomplished. You're doing good, Ikee."

Isaac smiled at the name only his family still used. He was a grown man and no longer went by that name, but as far as Keith was concerned there was only one Isaac, so he would be Ikee to his Unc and be okay with that. "Yes, but they are giving us the airtime because of the sermons Dam preached on their network a year ago. One of the executives told me that they were flooded with letters and donations to the network after Dam's sermons."

"I think I remember that. I wasn't feeling so well, so Cynda and I skipped church one Sunday. I decided to do a little bedside baptist, so I turned on the Christian station. I expected to see Bishop Thomas, but instead got a pleasant surprise when this young, and full of fire preacher stepped to the podium and preached his heart out."

"To be quite honest, Unc Dam is a better preacher than I am. He is truly anointed by God."

"You're anointed by God, and don't you forget it," Keith admonished.

Shaking his head, Isaac said, "You don't have to worry about that. I'm not ever forgetting who I am and what I'm called to do again in life. But, the special thing about Dam is that he has never strayed from God's calling. He has lived a pure life, and God is going to do a mighty work when the two of us get these revivals back on track."

"It still doesn't sound to me like you've got a problem." Keith picked up his iced tea and sipped.

"Dam's wife is pregnant, she's been put on bed rest. Money is tight for them, and Bishop Thomas is threatening to fire Dam if he does the revival with me."

Putting his drink down, Keith grinned. "Now that's a problem."

"See what I mean… why do I keep running into all these roadblocks? I thought doing work for the Lord would be easier than this."

"Boy, you know better than that. Satan is not about to sit back and let you snatch souls out of darkness. You are going to have a fight every step of the way. So, you've got to figure out if you've got what it takes to finish the job."

Isaac knew why Keith was asking such a question. After his parents died, Isaac had gone through a depression that was so severe at times, that he didn't even want to get out of bed in the mornings. If anyone had told him he would miss his parents so much, that he wouldn't be able to function, Isaac would have called them a liar. "I've got what it takes, Unc. Don't forget I'm Isaac Walker's son.

"No, don't you forget that you're Isaac's son, my nephew and most importantly a servant of God."

"I hear you Unc. I got this, I promise. I just don't know what to do about Dam and his issue with the bishop. I can't just tell him to quit his job when his wife is off work and dealing with a high-risk pregnancy."

"Bishop Thomas reminds me of a bishop your father and I used to work for. Did your father ever tell you about Bishop Sumler?"

Isaac shook his head.

Keith smiled as memories danced in his head. For the next hour, Isaac sat with Keith and listened to him talk about the good old days. When Keith finished traveling down memory lane, it was time to leave, everything in Isaac wanted to stay planted in his seat. This was the place he came to hear about his mom and dad. He'd left home after college to make his own way in life but discovered that he had spent too much time away. Now, he was a grown man, with a wife and a child but no parents to share their child with.

Isaac had allowed the sadness he felt for not being able to do another revival with his father to stop him from doing God's work altogether. Now that he was finally on track, he wasn't going to let anything get in his way, not even Bishop Thomas.

4

Dam was in the kitchen washing dishes when the doorbell rang. He dried his hands and went to open the door.

Amarrea yelled from upstairs. "Who is it?"

"I don't know. I'm on my way to the door now." His wife being laid up and unable to do much for herself revealed just how impatient she was. She had him running around here like a chicken with his head cut off making sure everything was the way she wanted it, so she wouldn't get out of bed and do it herself.

Looking out the peephole, a smile spread across Dam's face. He swung the door open. "Don't tell me you brought food," Dam said as he looked at the casserole dish his mother had in her hand. And the pot that his father was holding.

Demetrius and Angel stepped inside. Angel handed her dish to her son. "Hold this one, I've got a couple more things in the car."

Demetrius laughed as Angel made her way back to the car. "You know your mother. She can't sit still. Always has to be helping the needy and right now, you and my daughter-in-law are the needy."

"I can't argue with you on that. I was just in the kitchen washing the dishes trying to think of something to fix for lunch."

"Well, your mama has lunch and dinner covered for a few days." Demetrius put his pot on the stove and then went out to the car to help Angel bring in the other dishes.

"Okay, I made spaghetti, salad, soup and that tuna noodle casserole that Amarrea loves so much. And don't worry Son, I used very little salt in these dishes."

"She made y'all a cake in case Amarrea was craving something sweet." Demetrius took the lid off the cake dish and let Dam see the Carmel Bundt Cake. Another of Amarrea's favorites.

"Has she eaten yet?" Angel asked.

"No, ma'am." I was just getting ready to put something together."

"Let me take her some of this casserole and a piece of that cake. That'll put a smile on her face." Angel made the plate and then headed upstairs.

Dam leaned against the counter with a grateful expression on his face. "I can't tell you how much this means to me."

"Boy, don't think we don't remember how you burned them boiled eggs."

"I was ten, Dad."

"And you almost burned our house down. We haven't forgotten."

"So, Mama fixed all this food so I wouldn't burn this house down, huh? You know y'all wrong for that." Dam couldn't help himself, he chuckled at the thought of trying to cook but starting a fire instead.

"But all seriousness, Son. We know you have a lot on your plate with getting ready for this revival. So, your mom and I want to help with Amarrea in any way we can."

Dam sighed, he was truly heartbroken over having to bow out of the revival and wished he could just erase the whole thing from his mind. "I haven't told Amarrea yet, so this is just between you and me." Dam lowered his head and shook it. Then looked back toward his father. "I told Isaac that I couldn't do the revival with him."

"No, Son… no." Now Demetrius was the one shaking his head.

"I don't have a choice, Dad. But you know what… the weird thing about it is that I keep thinking God wants me to do something big for Him, then something always shows up to block it."

"Did you think it was going to be easy?"

"I didn't think it would be this hard. I didn't think I would make so many wrong decisions."

"Listen to me, Dam. You are a servant of God. This has been prophesied over you even while you were in your mother's belly. All your life Satan has been trying to destroy God's plan for you. Don't let him win."

~~~

Marissa Walker spent the day taking care of her son. She then fixed dinner and kept watching the clock as time ticked on. Isaac had taken to coming home late and ignoring her like he was too tired after talking to everyone else all day long to have a five-minute conversation with his wife.

When they were first married, they smiled and laughed together. They took long walks and talked about the things they were going through with the loss of Isaac Sr. and Nina, his mother. She thought things were good between them. She thought that having their son would bring Isaac back from the dark place he had sunken to after losing both his parents.

For a while, things had gone back to normal for them. But lately, Marissa had begun questioning whether Isaac still loved her. He was distant and moody all the time. And now he wasn't even coming home on time. Junior fell asleep, so Marissa put him in his bed, then turned on the radio as she cleaned the dishes. But then Tina Campbell's song, It's Too Hard Not Too came on, and tears began rolling down Marissa's face just as they did every time she heard that song.

Yes, she admitted to herself, she was angry with her husband. He was being so senseless and selfish lately that she did feel entitled to her anger. But Tina Campbell's song kept telling her how hard it was to hold onto unforgiveness. She put the dish rag down and went to her closet. She got on her knees and poured her heart out to God. "I don't know what to do anymore, Lord. I don't even know if he loves me."

As Marissa cried, she heard a still small voice say, "Love him."

She didn't want that response from the Lord. She wanted Him to tell her that he would make Isaac behave more like a man in love. So, she said, "But he's not treating me right."

She didn't expect a response that time, she just wanted the Lord to know that things weren't right in her world and the treatment she'd been receiving from her husband was the reason. She needed someone to join in on her pity party. But instead, she heard that still small voice again say, "Love him anyway."

Marissa stretched out on the floor and cried. She didn't want to love on Isaac when he was acting as if she wasn't important to him. She wanted to give him an ultimatum… either act like the man she married or pack your stuff and leave. But God required something else from her. God required her to get over herself and give Isaac the love and support he needed while he worked his way through the darkness.

As she pulled herself off the floor, Marissa wondered where her love and support was going to come from… who was going to see about her while she was making sure her husband had everything he needed? It was times like this when she really needed a good pep talk from Nina. That woman, her mother-in-love truly walked with

God. She was the epitome of how a Christian woman should walk, talk, act... all of it.

Marissa truly understood why her husband would have battled with depression after losing both his wonderful parents in the space of a year. He hadn't spent much time with Isaac Sr. or Nina the last few years of their lives. He had been out in the world making a name for himself and trying to forget everything he'd known about the God his parents served. Then the reality of having older parents kicked him in the butt. Nina had been fifty, and Isaac Sr. had been sixty-three when their last child was born. So, it was no surprise that at thirty-five-years-old he was now living without his parents.

Marissa was here to help him through the pain, but she didn't understand why he'd started pushing her away. That was their new norm, and she didn't know how much more of it she could take. Were they roommates or were they husband and wife? She desperately wanted to challenge Isaac with that question, but the Lord had admonished her to treat her husband right, even though he wasn't treating her so right.

Hearing the kitchen door open Marissa wiped her eyes and then rushed out of her prayer closet. "Hon, is that you?" She called out as she headed down the stairs.

"Who else would it be, Marissa? You didn't expect our three-year-old son to put his key in the lock and open the door, did you?" He laughed at her.

That was the other thing. Isaac's tone with her was short and sarcastic lately. Taking a deep breath, she ignored the comment. "You hungry? I was waiting for you to get home so we could eat together."

"I could eat this whole kitchen right about now." Isaac sat down at the table and waited to be served. "Whatcha got?"

"I just made penne noodle with that white cream sauce you like."

Isaac perked up. "Does it have the chicken and shrimp in it?"

"You know it." She fixed their plates, then sat down at the table with her husband. After he said grace and they dug into the meal, she asked, "So what took you so long to get home tonight?"

"I needed to talk to uncle Keith so instead of ringing his phone I decided to stop by and see how he was doing."

"Ah, wow. I would have loved to visit with them. How are Keith and Cynda doing?"

"I just sat on the porch with Keith, so I didn't get a chance to see Cynda."

"Cynda came to the house to check on me and junior a couple of months ago. I really should return the favor. She reminds me so much of your mother. Those two women have unshakable faith, and I need to be around that."

With a look of agitation on his face, Isaac said, "Hon, if you don't mind, I'd really like to eat in silence."

He was doing it again... couldn't even spare a few minutes to talk to his wife. She'd had enough. "Maybe you'd like to eat by yourself as well." Marissa grabbed her plate and left the kitchen. This man was mistreating her for no reason, and the Lord admonished her to love him anyway. When would the Lord tell Isaac that he needed to treat his wife better?

5

Amarrea's feet were still swollen, just like her belly. She could only get up to go to the bathroom, and after just three days of this, she was not only irritable, she was emotional as well. So, when Marissa called complaining about Isaac, Amarrea wasn't interested in taking up for him tonight. "No he didn't. Girl, you good because I would have put that whole pot of pasta over his head."

"Don't think I didn't want to. But I was praying earlier, the Lord told me to be good to Isaac even though he wasn't being good to me. I flunked the test at dinner tonight because I could only hold my tongue for so long. I know my husband is going through something, especially with Bishop Thomas threatening to fire Dam if he participated in the street revival, but he doesn't have to treat me like I'm the enemy."

"Wait... hold up. What did you just say about my husband getting fired?"

Complete silence came from the other end of the phone.

"Fess up, Marissa. What's going on?"

"I am so sorry, Amarrea. You are already stressed enough as it is. I shouldn't have opened my big mouth."

"But you did, so tell me what's going on, because clearly, my husband hasn't told me a thing."

"Okay girl, but I don't need you getting angry and getting that blood pressure up again. So, you have to promise me that you'll stay calm."

Taking a deep breath, Amarrea nodded. "I can do that."

"Evidently Bishop Thomas is ticked off about the street revivals. He told Dam that if he went through with it, he could kiss his job at the church goodbye. So, for the past few days, Isaac has been scrambling, trying to figure out what he and Dam can do about this situation."

"When did all of this go down?" Amarrea wanted to know.

"I think it was the same day you went on bedrest… matter-of-fact, I know it was the same day. Because I was so worried about you, that I forgot to mention it to you then."

"So, my husband quit his job, and nobody says a word to me?"

"No, Amarrea. Dam didn't quit his job at the church. He told Isaac that he wouldn't be able to do the revivals with him. That's why Isaac has been running around here acting like he lost his mind."

"Marissa, let me call you back." Amarrea hung up the phone as she heard Dam coming up the stairs. All Dam ever wanted to do was follow after God. And he had told her that the street revivals was God's next mission for him. So how could he just quit on it?

"Hey, beautiful," Dam said as he entered their bedroom. He leaned over and gave her a kiss on the lips.

She loved the feel of his lips on hers. But she couldn't concentrate on that now. She was too angry with her husband to think sweet thoughts. "What have you done, Obadiah Damerae Shepherd?" She demanded.

"Uh-oh, I know I'm in trouble when you use my full government name." Dam sat on the edge of the bed. "What did I do?"

"You know what you did… and I can't for the life of me understand it." She paused, breathed in deep as if trying to calm herself. "Why did you back out of doing the street revivals?"

He looked surprised, then a knowing looked flashed across his face. "You've been talking to Marissa."

"Of course, I talked to Marissa. But what I don't understand is why my best friend knew that you were having problems at work before I did. Why didn't you tell me what happened?" She balled her fist and punched him in the arm.

"Ooouu." He rubbed his arm. "Girl, you got some hands on you."

"Good, now that I've got your attention tell me what's going on."

"Look, bae, you know me, so I'm not going to pretend like backing out on the revival was no big deal. And when Bishop said if I didn't back out he would fire me, I was tempted to quit. I even came home to talk to you about doing just that. But that was the same day the doctor put you on bedrest."

Amarrea couldn't help herself, she burst out laughing. She put her hand over her mouth trying to stop the giggles.

"Well, at least you're laughing rather than punching."

"I'm sorry." Still laughing, she managed to say, "I just pictured your face when you came home that day and found me in bed with my feet propped up. Now I know why you looked so sick when I told you I'd been put on bedrest. I thought you were worried about me, but you weren't worried about me at all."

"I was too," he protested.

"Okay, I'm sure you were a little worried about me. But you were also sick about not being able to quit your job so you could lay around the house while your pregnant wife supports you."

"When you put it like that, I do sound like a bum. Good thing I kept my job, huh?"

"No, it's not a good thing." Amarrea became serious again. "Giving up on the revival when you know it's what you're called to do tells me that you stopped trusting God."

He shook his head. "Never that. But I do have a family to think about now." Dam walked to the bottom of the bed, removed the covers and started rubbing Amarrea's feet.

"Ooh, that feels good." Amarrea closed her eyes and leaned back while Dam worked his magic on her aching feet. But then she caught herself just before drifting. "You're not getting off the hook that easy, mister. Your family wants you doing what you were born to do."

"You want this house too," Dam quickly reminded her.

Amarrea pulled her feet away from Dam as she sat up and looked around the bedroom. This was one of her favorite rooms in the house. From the trey ceiling above their bed to the sitting area where she placed a lounge chair that she had spent months searching for and the white furry rug she placed on top of the dark hardwood floors that had been installed in their bedroom the week before they moved in. She loved everything about her bedroom, not to mention the adjoining bathroom had a deep soaking tub and a walk-in closet. All the things she'd put on her wish list… but these were just things.

"I don't need this house, Dam. And our baby will be happy where ever we are. But you will never be happy if you give up on God's plan for your life."

Dam's shoulders slumped as he hung his head. "I don't know what to do, hon. I don't want to disappoint God, but I don't want to let you down either."

She put her arms around her husband, hugging him tight as she said, "I'm going to tell you the same thing you tell me whenever I have a problem that I've tried to figure out on my own… let's pray."

6

Now there was a day when the sons of God came to present themselves before the Lord and Satan came also. Seated on His marvelous throne of grace the Lord set his eyes on Satan and asked, "From where have you come?"

Satan answered the Lord, "From going to and fro in the earth and from walking up and down in it."

And the Lord said, "Have you considered my servants Obadiah Damerae Shepherd and Isaac Judah Walker Jr., that there is none like them in the earth. They are perfect and upright men, who fear God and hate evil?"

But Satan answered the Lord, "Do they fear God for nothing? Haven't You blessed the works of their hands and protected them on every turn? I almost caused Isaac to spiral into depression after he lost his parents, but you sent angels to defeat the imps I had assigned to him."

"Touch not my anointed and do my profits no harm."

"As you command, but that just proves my point," Satan reiterated.

"The revival Obadiah and Isaac are working on will bring many souls into My kingdom. You've been working hard to stop the revival, and I will not stand in your way. Do what you will, and My servants will find a way to do My will."

Satan gleefully asked, "I can do anything I want, and You won't stop me?"

"My servants will stop you… As I said, do what you will only do not touch one hair on their head."

Satan bowed to the Lord. "I won't have to touch them. But I promise, when I'm done they will curse You to Your face."

~~~

Dam and Isaac met for coffee. After getting scolded by Amarrea and his father, Dam realized that he needed to be a part of this revival. God was up to something, and for some reason he wanted Dam to be a part of it. So maybe there was some way he could help Isaac out that wouldn't get him fired.

"I'm glad you called, man. Things are falling apart on this revival, I'm hoping we can find a way to pull it back together," Isaac said as the waitress sat a coffee mug and crumb cake in front of both of them.

"Amarrea practically beat me over the head when she found out that I backed out." Dam took a sip of his coffee. "I want to partner with you on this revival, I really do. But, I need to keep my job for my family. So, I'm kind of stuck."

"Totally understand where you're at. I just wish I had taken your news better. I've been a complete bear to deal with all week. Amarrea might have wanted to fight you, but my wife isn't even speaking to me."

Dam took a sip of his coffee, then put it down. "I hate to hear that. We are trying to do good work for the Lord. It shouldn't be this hard."

Isaac shook his head. "I was just talking with my uncle the other day. He and my father used to handle these revivals, and he told me all kinds of stories about the obstacles they ran up against. So, nothing much has changed, we just have to figure our way around these issues just like my dad and uncle Keith did."

"I should have never accepted the youth pastor position at Bishop Thomas' church. Every day I'm there I wonder how I could have missed God on this assignment." Dam prided himself on following the lead of God. He wanted his life to be a living testimony and to always be in the will of God. So, how he found himself working for a man like Bishop Thomas, Dam just couldn't explain it.

"What if you didn't miss God," Isaac suggested. "What if God put you in that position just so millions of people could see you deliver those two sermons that was not only seen on a cable Christian television station but was also posted on YouTube. Last I checked those two messages had about fifty million views. Which is the reason we received so much interest from several networks wanting to televise our revival."

Dam looked doubtful. "Or Minister Vicki could have just made a mistake."

"Two Sundays in a row?" Isaac shook his head. "That's not a mistake, that's a God-ordained intervention."

"Okay, let's say you're right, then tell me why Bishop Thomas now wants to fire me if I continue working on the revival? Tell me why my wife is on bedrest and needs me to earn money to pay the bills rather than do the will of God? We may have coverage from the networks, but I won't be there."

"And if you're not there, most of the networks will probably cancel," Isaac finished the thought for Dam. "But I have an idea that just may salvage the revival and our mission for reaching a hurting world."

"I'm all ears."

Isaac leaned forward, put an elbow on the table. "When I was talking to my uncle the other day, he mentioned that he and my father dealt with an ego-driven bishop years ago. And as he laid out for me some of their exploits, an idea struck."

"I hope it's a good one," Dam looked as if he didn't have faith in anything changing Bishop Thomas' mind.

"You just bring your lunch to work with you tomorrow. Be in your office around noon, and I will show you how we are going to deal with the good bishop."

~~~

"I knew you would come to your senses and get with the program," Bishop Thomas said as he playfully smacked Minister Vicki on her behind and then got out of her bed.

"You know I can't resist you. I want you here with me all the time. I can't wait until you get that divorce like you've been promising me." Vicki sat up in bed and pulled the sheet up to cover her naked body.

Bishop rolled his eyes heavenward like he was asking the Lord's help to deal with this wayward saint. "You're expecting too much from me, Vicki. My wife loves me, and she is beloved by our church members. I can't just break her heart like that."

"Then why did you come over here today?" Vicki's lip stuck out as she pouted.

"Because you called. I thought you were finally ready to accept your place. Plus, I haven't had much fun lately. I needed to be with you. Why can't you just be happy with what we have? You knew I was married when you laid down with me in the first place."

"Yeah, but you kept talking about how unhappy you were and how First Lady Jade doesn't care about you. Now you tell me that she loves you." Tears strolled down her face as she asked, "What am I supposed to do with that?"

"Take it for what it's worth. You and I had a good time. But maybe our relationship has run its course."

"So, just like that, I'm being dismissed. Do you really think I'm going to just take this and do nothing about it?"

"You can't hurt my ministry anymore if that's what you're threatening. I already had you thrown off the media team. So, Dam's messages won't be, he did quote marks in the air, 'accidentally' uploaded on any of the networks again."

"I can tell First Lady what you've been doing behind her back. You won't divorce her, but that doesn't mean she won't divorce you… because baby, I've got a serious story to tell."

"That is why I told Jade to get herself another armor bearer. I'm not about to let no devil in hell tear down what God has put together." Bishop snatched his clothes off the floor and headed for the bathroom.

"So, now I'm the devil? Just remember, you've been laying up with the devil if that's what I am."

"You're trying to bring down a man of God who has been anointed by the Almighty. God's word says touch not my anointed and do my prophet no harm. Now if you're bad enough to go against God, then like I said, you are a devil."

"Don't mess with me, Daniel." Vicki flung the sheet off and strutted over to him with a menacing look on her face as she put her full glory on display. "I'm the one you want. I'm the one you keep coming back to. But I'm telling you now if you don't make things right, I'm going to turn your life upside down. By the time I'm finished you're going to wish I was just the devil."

Grabbing hold of her bare shoulders, Bishop Thomas shook her. "It's over between us, Vicki. Go find some man to marry and leave me alone."

"I'll never leave you alone. You belong to me, and I belong to you."

"I belong to God."

Vicki laughed at him. He smacked her. Vicki stepped back, wiped the blood from her lip with the back of her hand, then smacked him back with her other hand. After smacking him, she lunged at his face, claws at him like an angry tiger.

He knocked her down, but not before she put a long gash on his left cheek. "You crazy. I'm getting out of here." Bishop Thomas quickly put his clothes on and left without showering.

7

Isaac glanced at his watch and became slightly irritated at the fact that Bishop Thomas was seven minutes late for their meeting. It wasn't that Isaac thought he was so important and should therefore not be snubbed in such a way. It was more that his father taught him that two things were important when beginning a business relationship… always be able to look a man in the eye and value his time.

Bishop Thomas was the one who asked for this meeting, Isaac had wanted this meeting and would have called the bishop himself because he thought that maybe talking to him man to man would help to smooth things over. But the fact of the matter was that Bishop called him, Isaac showed up, and the bishop didn't.

The church secretary had brought him into Bishop Thomas' office and seated him on the black leather sofa. She gave him a cup of coffee and a banana nut muffin while he waited. Isaac ate half the muffin, took a few sips of the coffee. As he glanced around, Isaac wondered about the square footage of this room. He'd been in big offices before, but nothing like this. Not only did Bishop Thomas have a sitting area with enough space for a sofa, love seat and an oversized chair, but there was also a long table that seated at least ten people for meetings or heck, Thanksgiving dinner if that's what he wanted to do. And if that wasn't enough, the bishop's desk was mahogany wood. It was so huge that it would take about six men to pick the desk up to even attempt to get it out of the room.

Glancing at his watch again revealed that Bishop was now ten minutes late. Marissa had asked him to come home for lunch so they could talk. He'd been in the doghouse with his wife for a few weeks now and did not want to stand her up. So, he decided it was time to leave. He'd get with Bishop another time.

Isaac walked out of the office and stood in front of the secretary's desk. He thanked her for the coffee and was about to reschedule the meeting with Bishop Thomas when the door opened, and the man in question rushed in.

"Isaac my boy, I'm so glad that you are still here."

"I was about to reschedule. My wife wants me home for lunch."

Bishop waved Isaac's comment off. "This won't take long at all. Come on into my office so we can talk. I'll have you home to your wife in no time."

"Sir, you're bleeding," the secretary said as she came from behind her desk to hand the bishop several napkins.

There was a bandage on his face, and his cheek appeared to be swollen. Isaac wanted to ask what happened, but it really wasn't his business.

Bishop held the napkin to his face. But he didn't thank his secretary for her concern. He glanced over at Isaac and said, "Come on young man. Let's have this discussion that should have taken place a year ago."

Isaac caught the shade the bishop threw at him. His nose crinkled as he itched to tell this man just what he thought of his actions. But he held it in because Isaac was here for Dam. That young man was a servant of God. And the Lord had need of him so Isaac would bow down to the bishop if that was God's plan. "I'm here now, so let's talk."

They went into bishop's office. He closed the door then offered Isaac a seat. "Let's sit over here." Bishop pointed toward the sitting area. Isaac sat back down on the plush leather sofa.

"I apologize for being late. I was out evangelizing this morning and got scratched by a wild animal. I ran back home so I could get bandaged up."

"What kind of wild animal attacked you?"

Bishop Thomas' eyes crossed as his hand swatted the air indicating the incident was no big deal. "Just a dog. I should have known better. That neighborhood always has dogs running around with no owners in sight."

"You probably should see a doctor. You don't want an infection to set in."

"I'll take care of that soon enough. Lady Jade will probably make me go to the hospital."

"My wife would probably pour a whole bottle of green alcohol on it." Isaac laughed thinking of how Marissa believed that green alcohol healed everything.

"Speaking of the wives… the next time your wife takes Lady Jade shopping, could you please tell her to stop my wife from buying the boutique out. My credit cards can't take many more of those shopping trips."

"I will tell her, sir." Bishop had married a woman twenty years younger. Jade was only a few years older than Marissa, and they enjoyed hanging out with each other from time to time. But Marissa never told him anything about extravagant shopping trips. "Now, let's get to it… you wanted to see me?"

"Oh, yes, yes." Bishop put a hand under his chin as he looked at Isaac as if studying him. It took him a minute to speak, but finally, he said, "God has put me in position to mentor young ministers so that men like you and Dam will be able to fulfill your God-given mission. So, I would be remiss if I didn't praise you when need be and correct you when that is needed also. Especially since your father is no longer with us, God rest his soul."

Isaac wanted to tell Bishop to keep his father's name out of his mouth. But he was disciplined enough to hold his tongue.

"Now, I can't help you young ministers unless you understand a few things first," Bishop began. "And first and foremost, I don't like when little upstarts like you and Dam think y'all just gon' use what God has blessed me with and not even reach back and say thank you."

On second thought… "Excuse me?"

"You heard me, and you know exactly what I'm talking about. How do you think your daddy would have reacted if some wet behind the ear youth pastor tried to steal his glory?"

Lifting a hand to halt the foolishness, Isaac said, "To answer your question about my father. The thing you need to know about Isaac Walker Sr. is that he never wanted the glory. He respected God too much to try to take what belongs to Him and Him alone."

"W-e-ll, well of course," Bishop stuttered. "Of course, the glory belongs to God. You misunderstood what I was saying. And I'm not going to let you turn my words around on me. Not when you and Dam have received very lucrative contracts from several television networks because of what I put in place.

"If I wasn't already paying several networks to broadcast my sermons, you and Dam never would have reaped the benefits of my stupid media manager's bumbling mistake. So, I think you owe a debt to me."

Isaac Jr. was the only child of Isaac and Nina Walker who hadn't lived in the hood. His mom had been a successful Christian fiction author and his dad a preacher of a neighborhood church, that didn't bring in a lot of money, but his speaking engagements and subsequent book deals garnered all the money he needed to live a lavish lifestyle.

But even though Isaac didn't grow up in the hood like his father and his siblings he still found himself on the street at the age of seventeen, bumping heads with drug dealers and killers, so this three-piece suit, toupee-wearing preacher, didn't move Isaac one bit. He sat up, cocked his head to the side and said, "Just what do you think we owe you, bishop?"

"For starters how about a little gratitude? If it wasn't for me, that kid wouldn't be getting attention from those networks. His association with this church made him a rock star... and now you and Dam just want to waltz off and act like he doesn't owe me anything."

Isaac had a whole lot he wanted to say. He was about to let loose on the bishop, but the secretary knocked on his door and then opened it. "Sir, Dam is here. He said you left him a message to come to your office when he finished with his youth meeting. Should I send him in?"

"Of course. He's the man of the hour, please send my protege in here."

Dam walked in. He and Isaac exchanged glances, then fist bumped. "Good seeing you, my brother," Dam said as he sat down on the sofa with Isaac.

"It's always good seeing you, bro." Isaac rubbed his hands together. There was so much he wanted to say right now. He was like his father in so many ways. He actually wanted to grab the bishop by the throat and choke him out. But that wasn't what Jesus would do. He had to let the Isaac Walker side of him decrease and allow God to increase at this moment. "Bishop and I were just talking about how we should show gratitude for all he did for us. I've been thinking about this myself, and I believe that we should ask Bishop Thomas to partner with us for this first revival."

Without thinking, Dam shook his head, "You don't have to do this for me, Isaac. If the bishop will not allow me to work with you this year, then maybe God has something else for me."

"Nonsense!" Bishop's voice boomed throughout the room. "I'm not going to let you shirk off your responsibilities like this. You gave your word to Isaac, and at Called of God we keep our word."

"But sir, I think it's best that I keep my job to take care of my family." Dam looked at the bishop as if the man had two heads and was speaking out of both mouths at the same time.

"Now see, it's that attitude right there. You have got to take the ministry serious, young man. I truly believe God has me mentoring you to light a fire under you. So, listen to what I'm saying, we will do this revival with Isaac, and I will make sure that all the networks cover it."

All the networks had already agreed to cover the revival, thanks to Dam's fiery sermons, but Isaac didn't feel the need to remind the bishop of that.

"Let's sit down here at the table so we can strategize." Bishop pointed to the table as he walked over to his desk. He picked up the phone and called his secretary. "Order us some lunch." He turned back to Isaac and Dam. "Turkey and ham sandwiches or fried chicken."

Dam sat down at the table. "A sandwich sounds good to me."

Isaac wanted to excuse himself. He should be at home having lunch with Marissa as he promised. But Marissa knows how important this revival is, and she knows that everything almost fell apart. Isaac wouldn't feel right if he didn't stay and finalize things with the bishop. "A sandwich sounds good to me too."

~~~

One problem solved, ninety-nine more to go. The next problem presented itself when Dam arrived home and heard sirens coming up behind him. As he got out of the car, he stood in paralyzed silence, watching as two EMTs rushed toward his front door, rolling a hospital bed between them. The front door flew open, and Dam saw his mother step onto the porch and hurry the EMTs into the house.

Somehow, his legs started moving, Dam didn't feel them moving, but they must have because he was no longer standing by his car. He was inside his house watching the EMTs place Amarrea on the ambulance bed. "What happened? What's going on?"

Angel ran over to her son and wrapped her arms around him. "I found her on the floor by the bathroom. She passed out."

"I knew I shouldn't have gone to work today." Dam held onto his wife's hand. "Baby, talk to me. How are you feeling?"

"Not so good... don't know what happened." Amarrea released his hands as her eyes slowly closed.

"We need to get her to the hospital," one of the EMTs told him as they strapped Amarrea to the bed and then rushed her out the door and into the ambulance.

"I'm coming with her," Dam told the EMTs as he jumped into the ambulance behind his wife.

"I'll pick up your father, we'll meet you at the hospital," Angel told her son.

Dam wasn't listening. He was praying. God had just opened one door by causing Bishop Thomas to allow him to take part in the revival. He thought he was coming home to tell Amarrea the good news, but instead, he was headed to the hospital as the EMTs worked to wake his wife back up and Dam needed God to tell him what in the world was going on.

~~~

At the same time that Dam was heading to the hospital, Isaac was headed for a disaster of his own making. "Why are you packing? Where are you going?"

Marissa kept her eyes on the clothes she was folding and placing in her suitcase. "I can't be here right now. I need some time to myself, so I can…" she trailed off, but kept packing.

"So you can what?" Isaac demanded.

Breathing in deeply and exhaling, Marissa turned to her husband. With the evidence of dried tears on her face, she told him, "I need to make decisions about my future."

"Don't you mean… our future. You, me and Junior. You can't just go off doing whatever you want without considering us."

She didn't respond. Marissa closed her suitcase and placed it by the front door. She then headed back upstairs to Junior's room and took his small suitcase out of the closet.

"Oh, so now you're going to take my son away from me too." Isaac shook his head. "Ah-ah, that ain't never happening."

"Don't you have work to do? Isn't this revival the most important thing in the world to you right now?"

"I never said that. You and Junior are the most important people in my life. Don't do this Marissa."

"I can't stay here. You have belittled me and made me feel as if I don't matter for too long. I have never been a bitter person, Isaac, you know that. But I swear I'm starting to resent you in ways that I don't know if we can recover from."

Her words hit and knocked the fight out of him. Marissa had been here for him through all of what he'd been dealing with. She had been the one he could count on to stay true and pull him up. Even on days when he'd felt too low to pray, Marissa had stuck by him, encouraged him to come up higher. He was finally getting back to normal only to discover that he had destroyed the one thing he needed like he needed to breathe. "What can I do, baby? How can I make this right?"

"Just give me some time."

"How much time, bae? What are we talking… a day… two."

Her cell phone rang before she could respond. She glanced at the caller info and then answered the phone.

"Hon, why you answer that? I'm trying to talk to you." Isaac paced the floor in front of his wife.

"Oh my God," She said as her hand went to her heart. "Is she going to be alright?"

"Who? What's going on?"

Marissa didn't respond to Isaac. She told the caller. "I'm on my way," then hung up. Turning back to Isaac she said, "That was Angel, Dam's mother. Amarrea has been rushed to the hospital." She reached for Junior getting ready to take him out of bed to put his clothes on.

"He's still sleep, hun," Isaac's voice was calm as he took Junior out of her arms. Go on to the hospital. I'll take care of Junior."

She started to object but thought better of it. "Okay, but I want to take him with me. So, I'll be back for him later tonight."

Isaac laid his son back down and then followed Marissa to her car. She tried to take the suitcase that she had set at the front door. But he told her. "This is the last thing you need to be concerned about. Go to the hospital and see about Amarrea and you can get your bags when you come back for Junior."

Nodding in agreement, Marissa got in her car and took off. Isaac remained in the driveway a few minutes after his wife drove off. He stood there praying for safe travels as she made her way to the hospital and a safe return home. He even prayed against every demonic force that was trying to tear them apart.

8

Dam was still in shock as he sat in the hospital waiting area with his family. Angel and Demetrius had gone to the chapel to pray. He was thankful that his parents were praying for Amarrea because he needed their support and he really needed to hear from God right now. His brothers DeMarcus, Dee, and Dontae were seated in the waiting room with him. The only one who wasn't there was Dodi, and that was because she now lived in New York.

Their beautiful sister Dodi was now a highly sought-after model who was not just a model earning top dollar, but she had also become an activist for prison reform and worked with Chaplins across the country to spread the good news of Christ. Dam was so proud of his sister. She had grown up well and had not only fell in love with the Lord Jesus Christ along the way but because of growing up in a crime family that was now reformed, she had a heart for those who still needed reform.

DeMarcus hugged Dam as he told him, "She's going to be alright, little bro. Get that worried expression off your face."

"I can't lose her, DeMarcus. I just can't." Dam understood that his words did not sound as if they were coming from a man who had stood firm in the confessions of his faith for most of his life. But at this moment, even though he trusted God with everything he had, he didn't know if the outcome of this situation would be the one he would choose. Right now, he wished there was some magical door number one and door number two that he could pick that would tell him how the rest of his life was going to be. But there wasn't, so all he could do was wait.

Dee got up, walked over to Dam, grabbed his hand and pulled him out of his seat. "Come on, man. I'm taking you to the chapel with Ma. You're not sounding like any brother of mine. If we have got to take you and drip you in some water to get you to trust God, then that's what we're going to do."

Dam was so impressed by the fire he witnessed in his brother's eyes that he agreed to go to the chapel. Of all the Shepherd children, Dee had been the most like their grandfather, Don Shepherd. The man had been a gangster and had once upon a time deemed the family business number running, pimping and drug dealing. But then Don's only son and heir to his empire met Angel. As the years went by, Demetrius began to see that the family business didn't have to be crime business.

Demetrius and Angel then set out to teach their children the precepts of God. They never wanted their children to be brainwashed as Demetrius had been, into thinking that a life of crime was their best and only option. Dee had been the only one who rebelled against his parents as he went to work for his grandfather in the crime business. But prayer and Dee watching his grandfather, the original OG accept Jesus Christ as Lord and Savior as he took his last breath convinced Dee to give God a chance.

"Why don't we all go to the chapel and pray," Dontae said as he stood.

But Dam shook his head. "I need somebody to stay here in case the doctor comes out with word on Amarrea."

"I got you, bro. I'll stay here." Dontae sat back down.

But while Dam and Dee were headed out of the waiting area, several nurses and doctors ran towards the double door entrance. As the doors opened, Dam could hear the voice over the intercom saying, "Stat… code blue."

Dee kept walking, but Dam stopped, immediately he knew something very wrong had happened to Amarrea. He had no time to walk all the way to the chapel. Dam prayed like there was no tomorrow right where he stood.

~~~

"She's coding." The defibrillator was put to her chest as they tried to shock her back to life. But a demon of death stood at the foot of her bed, encouraging her to give up the fight and just fall asleep.

Then a bright light illuminated at the head of the bed. The demon covered his eyes and backed away from the bed. "No," he hissed. "She's mine."

The angel of light shook his head. "You're too late. Don't you hear the saints praying? You will not win this fight."

"But she is my assignment," the demon complained.

"She was your assignment. She's mine now, the God I serve says that she will live and declare the glory of God."

The demon shrieked as his evil spirit form melted away like the wicked witch in the Wizard of Oz.

As the defibrillator was about to send shockwaves through Amarrea's body once again, the angel touched her chest with the palm of his hand as he bent over and breathed the breath of life back into her body. The doctors glanced at each other as the flatline on the monitor became wavy and mountainous again. "How'd that happen?" One asked because the defibrillator was still in his hands and had not been pressed to her chest again.

The other doctor shrugged. "Delayed reaction, I guess."

As Dam was getting off his knees, two security guards rushed over to him. "We received a report about a disturbance in this area."

Dam looked around. The area was quiet with only a few people passing by. "No disturbance here."

"Sir, let me be clearer," one of the guards said. "The report we received was that you were praying in this area and blocking hospital personnel from entering the emergency room through those doors." He pointed at the double doors directly in front of them.

"I didn't think I was blocking the doors. I was several feet away from them when I started praying."

"You do know that we can write you a ticket for trespassing and have the police haul you off to jail," the other guard said. His eyes filled with hatred for Dam.

"Hey, what's the problem here?" Dee interrupted the guards. "My brother's wife is in the emergency room fighting for her life, and the two of you want to harass him because he's praying for her? Y'all better back up before you get more trouble than you can handle."

"You threatening us? The guard unhooked his baton from the belt strap.

"Hold on, wait a minute." Dam lifted his hands to halt the confrontation. "We're just here for my wife. That's all."

"Back up, Dam. I got this." Dee stepped in front of his brother. "Give it your best shot, but just remember, if you get a swing, so do I."

"What's going on out here?" A man in a light gray suit stepped to them.

The guard's whole demeanor changed. The one with the baton clipped it back on his belt. "Hey, Mr. Matthews. We were just getting ready to escort these two troublemakers out of the hospital."

The man looked over at them. He then pointed at Dam. "Aren't you the youth pastor at Called of God?"

Dam nodded.

The man shook his hand. "I'm the hospital director. My name is Mark Matthews, my wife and I have been attending Called of God for a few months now. She insisted that we visit after we watched one of your sermons on YouTube."

"I'm glad to hear that. My wife was rushed to your hospital, I'm waiting on information from the doctor."

Mr. Matthews turned back to the guards. "Why don't one of you go back there and find out what's going on with Pastor Dam Shepherd's wife?"

Dee smirked. "We'd appreciate getting that information, rather than being harassed for praying."

"Who's harassing you for praying?" Mr. Matthews eyebrow lifted.

"Sir," the guard hurriedly pleaded his case. "We received complaints. We were just doing our job."

Mr. Matthews shook his head. Then angrily pointed toward the emergency room. "Do the job I asked of you and stop treading on people's first amendment rights."

"Yes sir, we're on our way." The guards left.

Dam thanked Mr. Matthews and then sat down in the chairs closes to the emergency room doors and waited for the guards to bring him word on Amarrea.

Dee sat down next to his brother and asked, "Why'd you stop and start praying in the middle of the hallway? I thought we were going to the chapel to pray with Mom and Dad?"

"It felt to me as if Amarrea needed me to do something right then. The only thing I could think to do was get down on my knees in front of those emergency room doors and pray." Tears were streaming down Dam's face, he wiped them away. "I wasn't trying to cause any problems, but Amarrea's need was urgent."

Dee was overcome with emotion as his eyes filled with tears. He put an arm around his baby brother. "You're my hero, you know that?"

Laughing, Dam reminded him, "I thought Pop-Pop was your hero?"

"Well, after him, you're my next hero."

9

"What is going on, Lord? Why is so much coming against us?" Isaac paced the floor as his son slept. He kept talking to God because he didn't understand why he was now separated from his wife while Dam's wife was in the hospital fighting for her life.

As Isaac continued to pray, revelation came to him, and he knew for sure that an enemy had done this… but not just any enemy. This enemy had supernatural powers to affect situations and circumstances that mattered to Isaac and Dam. He lifted his head heavenward and asked his Lord, "Why have you allowed the enemy to attack us like this? What can we do to stop him?"

Isaac knew that he'd asked two separate questions without waiting for a response to the first question. He stopped pacing the floor and stopped talking. He got down on the floor waiting and listening for that still small voice to guide him through the madness that had become his life. God was faithful, this Isaac knew. He no longer had an earthly father or mother he could turn to when times were tough. But he still had his heavenly Father. And Isaac knew that God would never leave him nor forsake him. He just had to wait and listen. God would show him the way.

Isaac didn't know how long he'd been sitting there, but somewhere in the space of time he clearly heard the words, '**his time is short… resist**'.

And there it was. God had spoken. It took Isaac a minute to understand what the simple words meant. But as he put it together, he realized that God was telling him that Satan had ramped up his attacks because God was about to put him in chains. Then the devil would not be able to trouble God's people for a long time to come. But for now, God was telling him to resist the devil, because in so doing, the enemy would have to flee.

Isaac wasn't going to let the enemy destroy his marriage and break up his home. Isaac and Marissa belonged together. As he looked back over the last couple of years, he could see the build-up of frustration in his wife's eyes every time he said something she didn't like. Or when he'd been more focused on the work of the ministry rather than loving the woman God had given him. He owed Marissa an apology, and she was going to receive it tonight.

Leaving Junior's Black Panther pajamas on, Isaac grabbed his keys and left the house.

~~~~

Angel and Demetrius were back in the waiting room with the rest of the family. Marissa was now seated with them as well. The doctor had just come out to speak with Dam and the family, they were still in shock at what he had said.

"I absolutely, cannot believe that Amarrea almost died back there. Now I know why your dad and I felt so strongly about going to the chapel to pray." Angel said as she put a hand on top of Dam's hand.

"Thank you for doing that," Dam said.

Dee pointed toward Dam. "We were headed to the chapel to pray with y'all, but then Dam suddenly dropped to the floor in front of the emergency room doors and starts praying. I'm telling you, this guy has some sort of hotline to God… I swear he does."

"How did you know to stop and pray at that very moment?" Demetrius asked Dam, eyes wide with curiosity.

"I don't have a hotline to God like Dee thinks." Dam tried to laugh at the comment, but the sound came out hollow and void of the kind of emotion necessary for laughter. "I've just learned to listen to the whispers in my head. And I heard the word 'pray'. To me, it felt as if the need was urgent, so I had to pray right where we were."

"The security guards tried to throw us out of the hospital," Dee told the group.

Marissa rolled her eyes heavenward. "For praying? What's wrong with people."

"I don't understand it," Dam said. "But their eyes were so full of hate... like they hated me because I believe in God."

"That's the world we live in now, little brother," DeMarcus spoke up. "I see it all the time. People don't want to hear about God these days. They want to do what's right in their own eyes."

"I dated a girl who told me that God interrupts her flow," Dontae, who had been quiet up until now said.

Angel cut her eyes at her son. "I hope you're not dating this girl anymore. I certainly don't want any of my grandchildren growing up thinking like that."

"No, Mama, I'm not dating her anymore." Dontae nudged Dee as he mumbled, "I should have kept my mouth shut."

Angel was about to say something else to Dontae, but at that moment a nurse rushed over to Dam. "She's asking for you."

Dam jumped out of his seat. "I can see her now?"

The rest of the family stood up. The nurse stopped them. "Only one person for now."

Demetrius put a hand on Dam's shoulder. "Go see about your wife, Son. We'll wait out here for you."

~~~

"What are you doing here?" Marissa asked Isaac as she took her son from him. "And why is he in his pajamas?"

"I was in too much of a rush to change him. I need to talk to you. But first, tell me how Amarrea is doing?"

"I don't think we will be able to see her tonight. But they let Dam go to her room. We just have to keep praying because she almost died tonight."

"I will pray. God's got Amarrea. So, don't worry okay."

She adjusted Junior on her hip. "I'm trying not to worry, but this caught all of us off guard. I have to admit I'm still a little shaken by the reports we received from the doctor earlier. But I calmed down a whole lot once she woke up and asked to see Dam."

"That's good." Isaac stood there for a moment, gazing at his wife. This beautiful woman he married and promised to not only cherish but love her like Christ loves the church. He'd allowed the cares of this world and the ministry to steal his joy. And once his joy was gone, he couldn't truly love his wife as she deserved. But all that ends now. "Can I talk to you for a few minutes?"

"Okay, but let's go to your car, so people don't have to see my son out here in his PJs."

"He's my son too," Isaac protested.

"Then why didn't you put some clothes on him." Marissa was irritated, and it showed.

"Let me hold him." Angel opened her arms to the little man, and he came right to her.

"Are you sure?" Marissa asked, not wanting to burden the Shepherd family when they were already dealing with so much.

"I'm positive. You two go on about your business and let us watch this child."

65

Marissa and Isaac left the waiting area and walked down to the cafeteria. As they sat at the table with some peach cobbler and hot coffee, Isaac got to it. "I was wrong, Marissa. I have neglected you and talked to you in ways that I am ashamed of. You deserve so much better than what I've given you."

"I know I do. That's why I left."

"I completely understand." Isaac didn't want to argue about anything, he just wanted his wife back. "I would have left me too. But believe me, I didn't miss our lunch today on purpose. Dam and I were taking care of something with Bishop Thomas."

"You think I'm upset just because you couldn't come home for lunch?" Marissa shook her head.

"No, I know it's a lot more. I started praying after you left, the Lord opened my eyes to what's been going on."

"And…" Marissa motioned her hand as if rushing him to get to the point.

"I have a clear understanding now… the devil is on assignment to destroy our lives, and I have been allowing him to do just that. But no more. I'm reclaiming my life, right here and right now."

"And what about the depression?"

"What depression?" Isaac looked around as if trying to figure out what she was talking about.

Balling her fists in frustration, Marissa almost screamed at him, "Isaac Judah Walker Jr., don't sit there acting like you haven't been dealing with depression. Remember, I live in the same house with you."

"Calm down, hon. I'm not pretending anymore. Yes, my parent's death took a lot out of me."

"I know it did," she was more compassionate now.

"But my parents are in a better place. And I can celebrate their life by following in their footsteps. So, from this day forward I only want two things… to do the will of God and to love my family."

Tears stung Marissa's eyes. "Do you mean it, Isaac?"

"I'm just speaking words here, Marissa. But come back home and let me show you how much I mean every word I'm saying. If I have to stop doing the revivals in order to get my family back, then I'll let it go. You just tell me what you need from me."

Marissa couldn't be so selfish as to ask her husband to stop doing something that she believed was ordained by God. Because she herself had attended one of those street revivals that her father-in-law had done. She lost something very important to her at that revival, but she'd gain so much more…

Marissa was so excited when Pastor Isaac invited her to the revival that she rushed to get dressed. She would have run to the car if she wasn't carrying baby weight, because all she had been doing was sitting in the house, staring at the paint on the walls.

"I am so glad you thought about me, Pastor Isaac. I wasn't doing a thing but sitting around watching re-runs of Law and Order."

As Isaac pulled up to a red light, he looked over at her, praying that the Lord would allow him to see into Marissa's heart, mind, and soul. He didn't know for sure if she was the right girl for Ikee, but he had a feeling that she was in their lives for a reason. "You know… Nina and I could always help out with some babysitting if you want to go back to school."

"I've been thinking about it," she admitted. "I just don't want to be a burden to anyone. And I really don't want to give Mrs. Nina another reason to dislike me."

"Nina doesn't dislike you," Isaac said quickly.

Marissa didn't believe it. In fact, she understood why Ikee's mother would be down on her. If her son brought home some random woman, saying he was in love and wanted to get married... oh and by the way, the woman I'm marrying is pregnant by another man. Yeah, Marissa would have a problem with that.

But because of Ikee, Marissa had changed. She wasn't the same person who dated drug dealers and held their illegal drugs and guns. The power of God had changed her, and she wanted Ikee's parents to know that. "It's okay, Pastor Isaac. If Mrs. Nina gets to know me, she'll come to see that I'm not such a bad person."

Isaac smiled and patted Marissa on the shoulder as they pulled up to the location. "I'm looking forward to Nina getting to know you."

Marissa smiled back at him with joy filling her eyes. "Me too."

They got out of the SUV. Isaac walked toward the stage while Marissa decided to help the volunteers put the chairs out. If she could have done more, she would have, because Ikee had told her on numerous occasions how good it made him feel to be a part of something bigger than himself. These revivals were everything to him.

As she sat down in one of the chairs she helped put out, Marissa imagined herself helping out in all sorts of ministry related events. There was something in this world that she was good at, and she planned to figure out just what it was. She began to pray, "Thank you for allowing me to be here today. Let me soak in the message and help out where I can. I want to be used by You."

"Is this seat taken?"

Marissa heard the voice, but she hoped it wasn't who she

thought it was. She looked up and saw Dana Milner, Calvin's on and off girlfriend standing there. Marissa didn't know if she would have to go into a witness protection program to get away from these people. Ikee had told her that his dad's past kept coming back to haunt him; maybe she would just have to deal with the reality of her past and learn to live for the future. "Hey, Dana. I didn't expect to see you here today."

"Calvin asked me to come."

Calvin's brother was the father of the baby Marissa was carrying. Marissa hated that her child would be related to a man like Calvin Jones.

As Dana sat down next to her, Marissa noticed that she was carrying the same bag Calvin tried to get her to hold the night before. That bag had several guns in it. Were they planning to shoot the people attending this revival? *Lord, help me. I don't know what to do.*

~~~~

Isaac stood behind the podium, looking out at all the people who'd gathered under this tent to celebrate the Lord. Marissa was silently cheering for him. Ikee had told her how someone tried to destroy the tent and even left threatening messages. The enemy didn't want this revival to take place, but his mouth was being shut as pastor Isaac opened the Bible and began reading from Psalms 27:

The Lord is my light and my salvation; whom shall I fear? The Lord is the strength of my life; of whom shall I be afraid? When the wicked even mine enemies and my foes, came upon me to eat up my flesh, they stumbled and fell.

Though a host should encamp against me, my heart shall not fear: though war should rise against me, in this will I be confident. One thing have I desired of the Lord, that will I seek after; that I may dwell in the house of the Lord all the days of my life, to behold the beauty of the Lord, and to enquire in His temple.

For in the time of trouble he shall hide me in his pavilion: in the secret of his tabernacle shall he hide me; he shall set me upon a rock. And now shall mine head be lifted up above mine enemies round about me: therefore will I offer in his tabernacle sacrifices of joy; I will sing, yea, I will sing praises unto the Lord.

He closed the Bible and began speaking to the people from his heart. "In these last and evil days, we can't allow man to make us afraid and cause us to give up and run away from the work God has put before us. Our mission on earth is clear... it is to do the will of God, not the will of man. So, stand up and whatever you do, never be ashamed to name the name of Jesus Christ.

Marissa was soaking in every word. She had been afraid too many times throughout her life. Most of her fears came from living in an area that was infested with crime. But what Pastor Isaac was saying made sense. She could put her trust in God and let go of fear altogether, maybe then she could do the will of God.

Pastor Isaac sat down as three praise singers stepped forward and began singing. Dana chose that moment to get up; she seemed to be in a hurry, but Marissa noticed that she left Calvin's bag behind. She wasn't about to pick that bag up. What if a cop saw her with the bag and then asked to search it. She didn't know how many years she'd get for the possession of illegal guns, and she didn't want to find out.

Marissa got out of her seat and ran after Dana, but Dana was track-staring it down the street like she wanted to be anywhere but the revival. Being seven months pregnant, there was no way that Marissa was going to catch up to Dana. She stood and watched

Dana for a moment longer. That's when she noticed Calvin's black Lexus with gold rims pull up next to Dana. She jumped in the car, and it sped off.

If that was Calvin, Marissa wondered why he didn't send Dana back for that bag and why he sped off like somebody was trying to carjack him. That was when she remembered that Calvin had warned her that Ikee shouldn't attend this revival, as if something bad would happen. Now, she was very curious about that bag. What had Dana left behind? She knew that it wasn't drugs or guns—no way would Dana have left Calvin's stash.

Everything in her was telling her to run... get out while the getting was good. But Marissa hadn't called Ikee yesterday to tell him what Calvin had said to her, now she was feeling guilty. If something happened to these people and she did nothing to help, Marissa wouldn't be able to live with herself.

Marissa rushed back to her seat. She bent down, opened the bag and started screaming. Marissa took the bag and started running away from the revival, still screaming while carrying the bag she'd just looked into.

As Marissa reached the street, she threw the bag up in the air and then tried to run back towards the revival, but she fell down and then there was a loud BOOM!

Marissa had lost the baby she carried that day. But she had given her life to Christ and years later, she and Isaac Jr. had gotten married and now have a child of their own. No, she would not stop her husband from working on the revival. There were too many young girls out there like she used to be who needed to know about Jesus and His power to bring them out of whatever mess they'd gotten themselves into.

Tina Campbell was right, it is too hard to hold onto the pain... she needed to forgive her husband so they could move forward.

10

Things seemed to get back to normal. Marissa came back home. She and Isaac were once again committed to loving each other. Amarrea was just days away from having the baby. Dam refused to leave her side for a month after the scare she'd given him. But once Amarrea felt better, she pushed him to get back to work.

Dam and Isaac moved full speed ahead towards fulfilling their God-given assignment. Things were going smoothly, almost too smoothly. But then, one Sunday morning while Bishop Thomas was preaching a live sermon for the Christian Network Channel everything got turned upside down.

There was a commotion in the back of the sanctuary. Heads swiveled towards the back to see what in the world was going on. That's when everyone saw a church security guard trying to pull Minister Vicki Gray out the back door.

"How dare you!" She screamed at him. "I've been a member of this church for ten years. I pay my tithes. You can't just throw me out of here."

"Please don't make a scene, Minister Vicki. I'm just doing my job."

"No! No!" She kept screaming. "This ain't right, and he's going to pay for this."

A man who was bigger than the security guard stepped to him. "Let her go. I'm not going to stand by and let you treat Minister Vicki like this."

The guard loosed his hold on Vicki's arm. "Bishop told me not to let her in service today. But she won't listen."

The moment the guard loosed his grip Vicki took off for the sanctuary. Bishop Thomas was standing behind the podium. He lifted a hand, trying to get her to stop. "This is not the time, Minister Vicki."

She kept strutting towards him. "Oh, well when is the right time to let all the wonderful members of Called of God International Ministry know that the good bishop has gotten me pregnant and wants me to have an abortion?"

"What?… Dear Jesus!… I knew something was going on with them two," were just a few of the words that were shouted throughout the sanctuary after Vicki made her announcement.

"That's a bold face lie," First Lady Jade jumped out of her seat which was directly behind the pulpit and rushed at Vicki.

Bishop grabbed his wife. "No hon, she's not worth it."

"That's not what you said when we were making this baby," Vicki hollered up at them. "Now you standing here with your wife and in front of this church acting like I don't mean nothing to you… but you told me you were going to divorce Lady Jade."

"Divorce me!" Lady Jade turned dagger filled eyes toward her husband. "You told that hussy that you were going to divorce me?"

"He sure did. You don't understand him like I do. I'm supposed to be the first lady of this church, not you."

"You've been sleeping with my armor bearer? Is that why you told me to drop her from my team?"

"No, Jade. I told you what she tried to do." Bishop's eyes widened as he suddenly remembered that they were filming this portion of the service. He turned to the media team and signaled for them to cut the feed.

The media team was stationed in the balcony. One of the team members hollered from the balcony. "We're live, sir. We can't just cut the feed."

"Unplug it! Cut the line. Do whatever you have to do." Bishop was livid as he took his preaching robe off, threw it on the ground and then stormed out of the sanctuary.

"Where are you going? We need to take care of this now. My baby is not going to be born to a single mother."

"Oh yes, it will be. You done let the devil trick you if you think you're getting my husband." Jade swooped down on Vicki so hard that she knocked the woman to the ground. The two women then rolled around on the floor, pulling weave and scratching faces until security pulled them apart.

~~~

Instead of going out to eat after church, Isaac and Marissa came home and made a salad with grilled chicken. Marissa chopped the veggies for the salad while Isaac grilled the chicken on the George Foreman.

"You grill the best chicken," Marissa said as she plopped a cucumber in her mouth.

"Is it me, or this George Foreman?"

"I think it's the spices you use. Your grilled chicken is the best. It keeps me away from fried chicken."

"You see how I'm cheesing right? I'm over here blushing because my wife said something nice about my grilled chicken. How pitiful does that make me?"

Marissa scooped the cucumbers in the salad bowl and then walked over to her husband and planted a kiss on his cheek. "Not pitiful at all. You are an awesome man and a wonderful husband to help me with dinner. And I love you."

"I love you more, bae." Isaac took Marissa in his arms and showed her how much he loved her with the deep sensual kiss he planted on her lips. As they were coming up for air, the house phone rang.

"Let me go, man. I need to get the phone."

"Let it ring," Isaac told her as he went in for another kiss. But then his cell phone rang. He tried to ignore that phone also. But they called right back.

"It might be important." Marissa giggled as she playfully pushed her husband away. She then took his cell phone off the counter and said, "Answer it."

"Yes, ma'am." Isaac saluted his wife as if she were an army drill sergeant. Glancing at the caller ID, he said, "It's Dam. I wonder if Amarrea is having the baby." He took the phone out of Marissa's hand.

"See, I told you to answer the phone."

"Hey Dam. Is everything okay?"

"Man, things just got real crazy. Can we get together today?"

Isaac put the phone on mute. "It doesn't sound good, but I don't think he's talking about Amarrea. He wants to meet."

"Ask him if they've had dinner yet."

Isaac took the phone off mute and hit the speaker button. "Have you and Amarrea eaten anything yet?"

"No. I was just getting ready to fix us something when things went crazy over here," Dam said.

"We don't want you to leave Amarrea. Is it okay if Isaac and I bring dinner to y'all?" Marissa asked him.

"Sounds like a plan," Dam said.

When Isaac ended the call, he turned back to his wife. "Are you sure you don't mind. This was supposed to be our time. Just the two of us. And how often do we get my sister to babysit for us?"

"Not often enough," Marissa smiled. "But I'm okay, Isaac. Let's take this food over to Dam and Amarrea's. It'll be like a double date."

~~~

"Wait, what?" Was all Isaac could say when Dam told him what went down at Called of God church that morning.

"You heard right," Dam said as they broke bread together. "I didn't go to church today, because I wanted to be here with Amarrea. But I recorded the service thinking I would watch it later this evening."

"If you didn't watch it, how'd you know what happened? Did someone call from the church?" Marissa asked.

"Have y'all not had your television on today?" Amarrea asked.

Isaac shook his head. "After church, we decided to just do us. No TV, no videos, just us. We were having the time of our lives until Dam called."

"Well, the story broke on the local news and then it made it's way to CNN. Now Bishop Thomas is phoning into all the news shows trying to do damage control." Dam picked up the remote and turned on the television. "I recorded this one. Pay close attention to what he says just forty-five seconds into the interview."

Isaac's eyes widened. He turned to Dam. "Why would that idiot mention the revival at a time like this?"

"I couldn't believe it either. He got caught on TV with his wife and girlfriend fighting over him, and he thinks it's time to talk up the revival." Dam just shook his head.

"I can't believe Jade was brawling with some woman. That's just not her character." Marissa looked like she was trying to make sense of what she had just heard.

"Girl, they weren't just fighting. Weave was flying, and shoes were hitting people upside the head. It was a mess." Amarrea couldn't help herself, she started laughing.

"It's not funny. This is serious," Dam reminded his wife.

"I know." She tried to stop laughing, but couldn't as she told Marissa. "You should have seen the bishop high tailing it out of the sanctuary. I've never seen such a spectacle in all my life."

"You did say you recorded the service, right Dam?" Isaac asked.

"Man, it was hard to watch," Dam told him.

"If it's that bad, I don't want to see it," Isaac said.

Marissa interrupted him. "Speak for yourself. I want to see that footage."

Isaac gave his wife the eye. "As I was saying. I don't want to see it, but I need to, especially since the bishop is supposed to be working on the revival with us."

"I thought he'd have enough decency to bail out, but after hearing him talk up the revival. I don't think he's going to bow out gracefully," Amarrea told the group as she took the remote away from Dam and switched the channel to the recording of Called of God.

"What's that noise?" Marissa asked as they watched Bishop standing behind the podium beginning his sermon.

"You'll see, keep watching," Amarrea told her.

They didn't have to wait long before Minister Vicki Gray came storming into the sanctuary and told everyone that she was pregnant with the bishop's baby. "Now I see why Lady Jade beat her down. I would have done the same thing. And then I would have gone upside your head when I got finished with her," Marissa pointed toward Isaac's head for emphasis.

"You don't have anything to worry about with me, bae. I love you and God too much."

"You better," Marissa said.

"Yeah, you better," Amarrea chimed in as she glared at Dam.

"Hold on. How did this become about us?" Dam pointed between Isaac and himself. "We are men of God, remember?"

"Bishop's supposed to be a man of God too, right?" Amarrea shook her head. "I'm telling you, this is why I have such a hard time getting the nurses I work with to come to church. They think all preachers are scumbags."

"There are good men in the church and good pastors. Some of us truly want to do God's will. All I can say for those watching preachers is that they've got their eye on the wrong thing. Jesus is our salvation, and they need to be checking for what Jesus wants," Dam told them.

11

The next morning Dam and Isaac were seated in Bishop Thomas' office trying to convince him to stop doing media interviews and to please drop out of the revival. But Bishop was not having none of it.

"Why should I bow out? Don't forget that I'm the main event. If it wasn't for me none of these networks would be televising the revival, so don't think you're just going to throw me by the wayside because some delusional, lying woman makes false claims."

"Those false claims were shown on the CNC network, and they are now threatening to pull the coverage of the revival. So, should we thank you for that too?" Isaac said.

Bishop harrumphed. Then twisted his lip and scrunched his nose as if he smelled something foul. "You think I don't know what's going on here?"

Dam and Isaac glanced at each other as Bishop pointed a finger at them.

"Y'all don't think you need me. Since Dam here tried to steal the spotlight from my ministry, everybody's been excited to hear what he has to say next. But this boy would be nothing without me."

"I didn't try to steal anything from you, Bishop. I have done the job I was hired to do at Called of God and nothing more." Dam tried to remain calm, but fire was shooting out of his eyes.

"Look, Bishop," Isaac began. "The bottom line is, with these allegations against you, it would create too much of a spectacle for you to continue on our team. Don't you agree?"

Sputtering, Bishop hopped out of his chair and got in Isaac's face. "No the Sam-Hill I don't agree. I'm the reason we have the television coverage in the first place. Oh, you may think that Dam had something to do with it. But who do you think pays the bills for those broadcasts Dam went behind my back to do."

Dam didn't respond. Just shook his head.

"And what about the fact that Dam plagiarized my sermon? You don't have a problem with that, do you?"

"What?" Dam was out of his chair now. "What sermon of yours did I plagiarize?"

"You've been stealing my sermons the whole time you've been here. I should have fired you, but the Lord told me to let you stay so you could continue to grow."

Isaac didn't believe the Lord talked to Bishop Thomas at all… at least, not in a very long time. "If it is as you say, that Dam has been plagiarizing your sermons for a years, why are you just now mentioning this?"

"I didn't want to embarrass the boy. But while I'm doing these interviews to clear my name from that lying, vindictive so-called woman of God, I just might discuss this plagiarism issue as well. Just clear the air on everything." Bishop looked from Dam to Isaac. He then grinned as he added, "However, I could be persuaded to keep my mouth shut."

~~~

"Thank you for meeting me for lunch, Jade," Marissa said as the two ladies sat down.

"Thank you for inviting me. After what I did on Sunday, I'm being shunned by most of the first ladies in this city."

Marissa put a hand on top of Jade's to offer support. Jade was a beautiful woman, a Vanessa Williams look-alike with hazel eyes and all. She was twenty years younger than Bishop Thomas and his second wife. It had been rumored that bishop had cheated on his first wife while she lay on her deathbed with Jade. Hence the reason he married her six weeks after eulogizing his dear departed wife.

Marissa didn't judge Jade on that. She had skeletons in her closet as well. All the men in her life before Isaac had left her with scars, so she had no stones for her sister in Christ. Only love. "Girl, you know we are better than that. You and I will always be friends."

The waitress took their order then Jade said, "I know I could have handled things better. But Vicki took me by surprise. Believe me, I know that Daniel is a no-good cheat, but I had no idea he was cheating with my armor bearer."

"Do you hear yourself, Jade? You just told me that you know he cheats. Doesn't that bother you?"

Jade took a sip of her soda. As she put the glass back down on the table sadness crept into her eyes. "It bothers me. But do you want the truth?"

"If you want to tell it."

The waitress put their food in front of them. Jade pushed her plate away as she sighed deeply. "I was pregnant when I married Daniel. That's why we had a quick ceremony just six weeks after his first wife died."

Marissa gasped. Jade didn't have any kids of her own, and she had never been told about a pregnancy.

"I lost the baby the week before we were going to announce it to the church. I got pregnant again about a year later but had another miscarriage. After that, I didn't want to try anymore. Because you see, I think my barrenness and bishop's cheating are my punishment from God."

Marissa watched as tears escaped Jade's eyes and floated down her cheek. For years she had hung out with Jade. They'd shopped together, gone out to eat together. Attended church conferences together… and not once did Marissa ever realize that Jade was carrying such a heavy burden. "God's not punishing you, Jade. And He doesn't want you to punish yourself either."

"I don't know if I believe that, Marissa. If only you knew how awful I was to Daniel's first wife. I didn't throw our affair in her face or anything like what Vicki did to me. But I helped take care of her during her last days. I smiled in that woman's face all the while knowing I was sleeping with her husband. That makes me a bad person."

Marissa shook her head. "I never told you this, but I lost my first child too. I was pregnant by one of the neighborhood bad boys. When I lost the baby, I wondered if God was punishing me for having sex before marriage. But then I went to God about it, and I discovered this great big thing called forgiveness."

Nodding furiously, Jade said, "I've prayed and cried and begged God to forgive me for years now. I'm not the same person I was back then, Marissa. I truly love God. But…"

Marissa lifted a hand to stop Jade from saying another word. "There's no buts about it. You just said it, Jade. You're not the same person anymore. You're not a bad sinner. You are a forgiven person who sinned… catch the tense, because I just put that sin in your past. Will you do the same? Will you accept God's forgiveness for your sins?"

Tears were gushing down Jade's face now. She picked up her napkin and wiped her face as the tears kept coming. Taking a few deep breaths, Jade calmed herself down. She looked over at her friend as understanding filled her eyes. "All this time, I've been forgiven... all this time, God has been trying to love on me, but I've been the one pushing Him away because I didn't feel worthy."

"Look at you, figuring things out." Marissa got up from her seat and pulled Jade up from hers. She hugged Jade so tight like she was trying to get the woman to feel God's love from her hug. "You are special to God. Do you hear me?"

Jade nodded but kept holding onto Marissa.

"God wants the best for you, my friend. Stop letting people give you less than what God wants you to have."

~~~

"So that's it? We just let him get away with this?" Dam was so angry he wanted to punch the walls... or better yet, Bishop Thomas.

Isaac plopped down on the sofa in his office. "I messed up. I tried to handle Bishop the way I thought my father would have handled him. Thinking that we should invite the snake in to keep an eye on him."

"Men like Bishop Thomas need to be dealt with the Don Shepherd way." After saying that, Dam ran his hand over his forehead as if trying to erase some things from his memory bank. "I shouldn't have said that. When my grandfather had a problem, people usually ended up dead."

Isaac laughed. "That's the way my father handled his problems too. Then he met Jesus. And instead of taking a life, Isaac Walker, Sr. gave his life to bring thousands upon thousands of people to Christ."

"And that's why I'm so sorry that you asked me to help with these revivals. I feel like I'm destroying your father's legacy."

"Dam, don't be silly. How on earth could you be destroying my father's legacy?"

"You must admit that if I wasn't partnering with you, Bishop Thomas wouldn't have insisted on joining in. And we wouldn't be dealing with such a spectacle right now."

"And you have to admit that adding you has provided benefits for our mission," Isaac told Dam.

But Dam wasn't swayed. "What benefit I may have brought, Bishop is about to tear it all down when he goes on national television and claims that I've been stealing his messages." Shaking his head at the predicament. "I can't let your father's legacy be destroyed by this. Not by a man like Bishop. I'm going to bow out, Isaac. Maybe if I do that, the networks will stay with you and the revival will be everything God meant for it to be."

"No Dam. This is not what God wants." Isaac's head was throbbing. He put a hand on his temple and closed his eyes. Letting out a deep sigh, Isaac opened his eyes again. "God clearly showed me you when I began praying about this revival. My father didn't handle God's mission on his own. He had my uncle Keith right there by his side the whole way. But I believe there were certain things my dad couldn't do for the Lord because of the life he once led. I don't know what all we are meant to do... but I've got a feeling that God is taking us back to them Billy Graham kind of crusades."

"You think that many people will attend the revival?"

"Of course I do... why else would I have rented that football stadium? Not only are we going to fill up those bleachers, but we're going to bring in chairs and line that field with chairs as well. This is going to be an event even bigger than Joel Olsten's Night of Hope."

"Oh, you dreaming big like that. Then you definitely don't want me around messing up your flow." Dam said.

"That means I need you even more. God is doing great work in us. We can't let Bishop Thomas stop God's work."

"I hear you talking, my friend." Dam hesitated, for just a moment. "Let me pray on this."

"You do that," Isaac said. "God will show you that Bishop Thomas is just a distraction from what He is doing in the earth."

12

Dam went home and talked to Amarrea about everything he was feeling. He was unsettled in his spirit because he'd never dealt with so much turmoil when doing work for the Lord. Had he stepped into yet another thing that God had not called him too?

He was so despondent that he forgot all about praying. After dinner, he went into the family room with Amarrea and put on a movie. Needing room to stretch out, Amarrea laid on the sofa. Wanting to keep his wife comfortable, Dam picked up one of the blankets they kept in the family room and pulled it over her huge baby bump.

Dam took a seat on the recliner next to the sofa and leaned the seat back. "What do you want to watch?"

"I don't know… maybe a comedy. I think that's what we need right now," Amarrea said.

Yawning, Dam handed the remote to Amarrea. "See what you can find."

She began channel surfing. Dam caught the bits and pieces of the movie about a poor family struggling for a way out of poverty. The two sons chose a life of crime, and one of them was murdered. As he drifted off to sleep, he thought, no comedy… that's a tragedy.

His dreams weren't funny or kind either. As Dam drifted further, he felt as if he was walking through a movie scene. One character had gotten shot and was bleeding out. A paramedic tried to help him, but as Dam passed by them. Both the bleeding man and the paramedic turned to Dam and said, "Why didn't you help us?"

The question caught Dam off guard. He wasn't a part of this movie. What kind of help could he have given? As he continued further down the street, cameras rolled as a woman jumped off of a building. Dam shouted, "Stop!"

The woman who jumped had no safety net below her. Everyone just stood around either watching or filming the incident. Dam rushed over to the woman. Her lifeless body lay bloody and broken on the ground, but the people went on about their business as if nothing out of the ordinary had occurred.

He reached for his cell phone, figuring he should at least call the authorities. But he didn't have it with him. Dam turned to the people and hollered out to them. "Can someone help, can anyone call 911?"

"Man, why you acting like you care now? You left people like her and me to fend for ourselves, and that's what we're doing."

"What are you talking about? Isn't this a movie set? Why are people dying on this set?"

The man laughed at him and stumbled away as if he'd been drinking all day and could barely hold himself up.

As Dam looked around, it appeared to him that these cast of characters had no script. Everyone was just doing as they saw fit to do. There didn't appear to be any laws or right and wrong in this place. Sin had totally taken over, and no one seemed to care. He needed to get out of here. Dam started running, but it seemed the faster he ran, the worse things got. There was no way out of this God forsaken place.

He stopped running and bent over to catch his breath. But when he stood back up, Dam's eyes widened as he watched mummy like forms coming toward him. As they slowly moved toward him, Dam heard them say, "Why are you running away from us again? Why didn't you tell us? Why'd you let us die like this?"

"I didn't! I didn't!"

"Honey, calm down and wake up." Amarrea stood over Dam, nudging his shoulder.

Dam flopped and flipped in his chair. Amarrea kept nudging him until his eyes popped open. He laid there, staring at her as if he didn't know where he was. "What? What?"

"You're only dreaming, Dam. Stop looking like that. You're scaring me." Amarrea was concerned about her husband one moment, but the next moment a pain hit so severe that it doubled her over. She yelled out and then took deep breaths as the pain subsided.

Dam jumped out of his seat. He held onto Amarrea. "Baby, are you okay?"

"No! That was awful."

Dam helped Amarrea to sit down on the sofa. "Take a deep breath."

"I am," Amarrea screamed at him. She then put a hand to her head to wipe the sweat beads away. "I'm sorry. I didn't mean to snap at you."

"I've gotten used to it," Dam joked with her.

"It's not my fault. This pregnancy is not normal. I don't understand why I'm having so many problems. I'm a nurse, and I've tried my best to live a healthy life. So, I don't get why…" Another pain stabbed at Amarrea's core. She grabbed Dam's hand and squeezed until the pain subsided again."

"Ouuu," Dam complained as he snatched his hand from Amarrea's grip.

"Don't you dare complain about your hand when I'm suffering through this pain."

"Are you having contractions? Should we go to the hospital?"

Amarrea's eyes widened. She stared at Dam as a light bulb went on. "I didn't even think about that. I must be in labor. Praise Jesus!" Amarrea almost leaped off the sofa like she wanted to dance. "Let's get this party started."

"Wow, I didn't know the thought of labor would bring you so much joy."

"Are you kidding." Amarrea headed toward the stairs. "This whole pregnancy thing is about to be over. My baby is going to be here, and I won't have to elevate my legs, or sleep sitting up, or be rushed to the hospital as I pass out… It's over."

"Where are you going?" Dam asked as he grabbed hold of Amarrea's arm trying to slow her down.

"I'm going upstairs to get my bag. We need to get to the hospital."

"You are not climbing those stairs while you are in labor. Have a seat, I'll get your bags. Good lord, woman, show a little patience for once in your life."

"Hurry up. I'm ready to go."

Dam laughed as he rushed up the stairs. Never in his life did he ever imagine any woman would welcome labor. But Amarrea had been through so much while carrying their baby that he understood. His wife was going to have a baby. Dam only prayed that their child would never live in a world like he'd just been dreaming about, where everyone lived in sin and blamed him for their sins.

~~~

Dam was in fervent prayer for Amarrea as she endured labor like a soldier. He wanted God to ease her discomfort. But Amarrea told

90

him that labor was supposed to be uncomfortable. "This is the time when a woman feels great pain and great joy within moments of each emotion."

"I know honey, but you've gone through so much to carry our baby. It hurts me to see you in so much pain. I wish I could do something to help you."

"You can." She took a few deep breaths when I pain shot through her body, then said, "Your dream seemed pretty intense. Tell me about that."

He didn't want to think about that dream, let alone talk about it. But if it would help take her mind off the awful pain that continued ripping through her body, then he would talk about it. "It was one of the most terrifying dreams I've had in a long time. I thought I was on a movie set at first…"

When Dam finished telling her about that awful dream, Amarrea said, "God is trying to tell you something. Are you paying attention?"

"I'm trying," he answered honestly. "But there's been a lot going on."

"You don't have to tell me about all that's been going on." Amarrea pointed to her oversized belly and the IV she was hooked up to.

Dam smiled. He wanted to laugh, but he didn't have the strength. His stomach growled, he rubbed it, then asked, "Do you mind if I run down to the cafeteria and grab a bite to eat. I promise I won't be long. But I need something in my stomach."

"Take your time, it's not like I'm going anywhere."

"Yeah, but I want to be here when the pain hits so you can try to break my hand again."

"Don't be cute, because I just might do it," she warned.

He stood. "I wish I could bring you something back. I hate that they won't let you eat until you deliver the baby."

"Don't rub it in, husband. Just go get something to eat and get back here so I can hold that hand of yours." She gave him a sinister glare, and he hid his hand and backed out of the room.

Dam headed to the cafeteria thinking about the child that was about to be born, and praying that his wife's suffering would soon be over. He'd never imagined the dangers that women deal with while carrying a child. After this, he wasn't sure if Amarrea would want any more children, but whatever her decision, he would honor it.

He had his head down as he was in deep thought, he didn't notice the man in the dark trench coat with a big flopping wet hat approaching him. But when Dam looked up, his first thought was to wonder if it was raining outside. It hadn't been raining when he brought Amarrea to the hospital, and he didn't hear any rain beating down on the building.

The man stopped in front of Dam. Dam was about to go around him in an attempt to avoid an unwanted confrontation. But something in the man's eyes caught Dam off guard. Before he could move out of the way, the man put a hand on his arm and said, "Thus says the Lord, we have entered the last dimension of warfare. God has anointed you for such a time as this. Be bold and speak the truth to those who refuse to hear it. For the time is near."

The moment the man touched his arm, Dam felt hot all over, as if fire had shot through his body. The man released him and walked away. "Wait, what is this last dimension your talking about?"

The man kept walking. Dam tried to catch up with him. But a door opened, and hospital personnel rushed out of it as if their shift had just ended and they wanted to get out of here before an emergency occurred and they would be forced to do another shift.

Dam could understand their urgency, but they were in his way. He tried to move through the crowd, but it was no use. The man who had prophesied to him was gone.

Turning back around, he headed once again for the cafeteria. Dam purchased a sandwich and his favorite coconut pecan cookies. He put the cookies in his pocket, ate the sandwich, then rushed back to Amarrea's room. The whole while, he kept thinking about what the prophet said to him. Amarrea had asked him if he was paying attention. If he wasn't before, he certainly was now.

As he opened the door to Amarrea's room, he was fully prepared to tell her about his encounter, but the fact that his wife's legs were now in stir-ups, and the doctor was standing between her legs as she was screaming her head off, caused him to forget about retelling that incident.

He rushed to Amarrea's side feeling a bit guilty for chasing after that prophet, instead of going straight to the cafeteria and rushing back here. "We're having the baby now?"

"No joke," Amarrea snarled at him as sweat beads danced around her forehead. "What took you so long?"

"I'm sorry honey. I didn't think you were ready to deliver." He took a few napkins off the nightstand and wiped the sweat from Amarrea's forehead. "I'm here now. And I'm ready to help in any way I can."

She screamed again. The doctor said. "The baby is coming. Take a few deep breaths then I need you to give a big push."

"I don't want to push," Amarrea complained. "It hurts!"

"You can do this, babe. Breath." Dam coached.

Amarrea panted as another sharp pain hit her.

"Push!" The doctor ordered.

Dam gave Amarrea his hand. "Go ahead, hon. Take my hand. Squeeze it as you push."

The heart monitor started beeping. "The baby is in distress. We need to get going," the doctor admonished.

"You can do this," Dam once again offered his hand to his wife.

She grabbed hold of it. Squeezed and pushed... pushed and squeezed.

"The head is out. Now let's give it one more big push," the doctor said.

"You're doing it, Amarrea. Our baby is almost out. Just one more push honey."

Amarrea released Dam's hand as her eyes fluttered. "I need a nap," she said.

He wanted to laugh. But looking at her, Dam could tell that his wife didn't have much strength left. If he could push this baby out for her, he would... well, maybe not. But he did hate that she was suffering like this. Dam bent down and whispered in her eye. "God's got you, babe. You're going to get that nap, but first, we need one more push."

She nodded, then lifted her upper body off the bed. She took a deep breath as Dam wipe sweat from her face and then hunched down and pushed. Amarrea then laid back down and asked, "Can I take my nap now?"

The cry that Dam heard at that moment, took his eyes off his wife and centered them on the beautiful baby the doctor held in his hand.

"You've got a girl," he told Dam.

"Yes, I do." Dam had the biggest smile on his face as he glanced back at his wife. She was sleep.

13

Lady Jade woke up with a made up mind. She was not going to take Bishop Daniel Thomas' mess anymore. She took two empty boxes out of the garage and walked back up to her bedroom. One by one, she opened the dresser drawers, taking ties, underwear and dress shirts out of them and throwing them in the boxes.

She then started on their walk-in closet. The good bishop had more clothes than she did. Always talking 'bout he had to look good and couldn't keep wearing the same suits because of the position he was in. Like wearing a clean suit would save a soul. He should try having a clean heart.

"What are you doing?" Bishop's voice was like a loud thunderous boom in the confines of the walk-in closet.

Jade jumped and dropped the suites that she had just taken down. "Why would you come in here yelling like that. You scared me."

"You in here boxing up my clothes and want to know why I'm yelling. Woman, you must be smoking, and I don't mean them cigarettes that you sneak out back to puff on." He picked his suits off the floor and attempted to hang them back up.

"Least I'm not sneaking around having sex with anyone who wants it. I have upheld my marriage vows." She pulled another suit off the hanger and threw it at him.

"Don't think you're so perfect just because you haven't cheated on me. Because you sure laid down with me when I was married to my first wife. And then you even had the nerve to slither in my house, like the snake you are and take care of my ailing wife."

An outstretched finger pointed directly at his forehead, as she declared, "You don't get to hold that over my head not one more day. God has forgiven me for what I did. And you best believe that being married to you and taking your mess for all these years is my atonement for my sins."

"Paaa-lease," the bishop scoffed. "You've had it good as my first lady. Don't you think for a minute that another woman wouldn't love to take your place."

"She can have everything you ever gave me. I don't want it. I'd rather have peace of mind and you as far away from me as you can get."

"Well if you don't want anything from me, why aren't you packing? Why are you packing my clothes?"

"This house belongs to the both of us. My name is on the deed just like yours. And you have got to go." Jade walked out of the closet as she said, "Matter-of-fact, you can pack your stuff yourself. And if you don't want to do it, you can hire a professional moving company."

"So, you're just going to leave my clothes on the floor like that?" Bishop followed Lady Jade into the bedroom with a look of bewilderment on his face.

"Yes, sir. I'm done taking care of you. Get one of your girlfriends to come to pack you up. I just don't care anymore." She shrugged. "Do whatever makes you happy."

"Being here with you makes me happy." He stretched out his arms, approaching the bed as if trying to hug her.

Jade shook her head. "You need to find your happy place somewhere else because I'm done."

Anger flared in Bishop's eyes, as he exploded. "You can't put me out of my own house!"

Jade folded her arms across her chess and sneered, "I have you right where I want you, Mr. so-called Bishop. Just remember, I know how much of the church money we used when we bought this house. I know how you purchased that Lamborghini. And I know about all the other women you have used and abused at the church."

"Wh…wh," he sputtered but couldn't quite get words to form.

"I can have you arrested and get you thrown out of that church you think you own. So, don't mess with me."

Finding his words again, Bishop said, "How is it going to look if you throw me out like this?"

"I'll let you work that out. But if you leave this house, I won't divorce you right away. You can tell the church folk whatever you want about me. Maybe, I've lost my mind, maybe I'm going through a mid-life crisis and just don't want to be married anymore. Tell them that we're in counseling. You can act as if you've tried everything in this world to save our marriage and then when I divorce you in the next three to four years, you should be fine."

"I don't want a divorce. A man of God should never even entertain such a thought. Maybe we really should go to counseling. Maybe, if you give us some time, we can work through this."

"Pack your clothes, Bishop." Jade strolled out of the bedroom without so much as a backward glance.

~~~

"The revival must go on. God revealed that to me, and I understand what I am supposed to do now," Dam told Isaac as they stood in front of the hospital window viewing his baby girl.

97

"Right, but remember, this is not just a revival anymore. We are on a crusade to bring souls back to Christ. That was clearly revealed to me. God even showed me that I am to preach a message on forgiveness because the peoples' hearts have grown cold because of unforgiveness," Isaac said.

"God has been working on both of us. So, now all we have to figure out is what we're going to do about Bishop." Dam's stomach turned at the thought of doing this crusade with a man like his boss.

"Let's just admit that Bishop has us between a rock and a hard place right now," Isaac said. "But we serve a God who is well able to remove any and everything that is in our way. We will just move forward and trust God to handle the good bishop."

Dam nodded. "I've got more important things to think about anyway… like what to name this beautiful princess."

"You and Amarrea haven't picked a name yet?"

Dam smiled. "I haven't been able to convince Amarrea to go with the name that I want yet."

"What name did you come up with?"

"I want her to be named Esther."

"I get it, bro. Like the Queen who delivered her people from their enemy." Isaac said.

"See, you feel me, right?"

"Yeah, I feel you." Isaac put a fisted hand to his mouth and laughed. "But ain't no way you getting no modern day sistha to name her baby Esther. Good luck with that."

"Yeah, yeah, I've already been told to give up my dreams." Dam stared through the window at his daughter again. Honestly, he wasn't upset that Amarrea didn't like the name Esther for their daughter. He was just relieved to be able to look at his daughter and that his wife was doing well.

When Dam finally pulled his eyes away from his daughter, he said, "We have a month until our crusade begins and here I am with a baby."

"Take some time to be with your wife and your baby, my friend. I can handle the upcoming meetings."

"If you can give me a week or two to help Amarrea and make sure that she is alright, I should be good to go after that." No way was Dam going to go on as if it was business as usual after the ordeal Amarrea had gone through in order to birth their child.

"I got you," Isaac patted Dam on the shoulder as the two men walked back to Amarrea's room.

When they opened the door, Amarrea and Marissa were hysterically laughing. Amarrea was holding her stomach as if the laughter was causing her pain, but she just couldn't stop. "What's so funny," Dam asked.

Amarrea turned to her husband. "I just told Marissa how I fell asleep as soon as I pushed the baby out and didn't even see her until an hour later."

"It's true," Dam confirmed. "She was lights out. I'd never seen anyone fall asleep so fast."

"I'm going to try that same trick when we get home and see if I can get you to handle a few feedings."

Amarrea was in good spirits, and he loved it. "I was just telling Isaac that I plan to take a week or two off from work so I can take care of my girls. I think I can handle a few feedings."

"Wait a minute," Amarrea shook her head. "You have the revival coming up. You can't just take off as if you have nothing to do."

"Correction, it's called a Crusade now. And I plan to work on my speech while I'm off work, and Isaac is going to handle the meetings until I can catch up with him. We've got this covered, woman. So, let your man take care of you."

Amarrea glanced at Marissa. Her friend smiled at her. She turned back to her husband. "How can I refuse that. I guess I'm going to sleep for two weeks."

14

The first night of the crusade was a bit rocky. Since they were doing five nights straight, Bishop decided that he should preach the first and the third night because his sermons would get the crowd excited and bring in so much viewership that the networks would carry us each night of the crusade… according to the bishop.

Dam and Isaac kept praying as the evening of the first night rolled in, and the people began arriving. Another problem occurred when they discovered that Bishop had instructed his team to make the first fifty seats on the field VIP seats. However, only the front row had been blocked off for Dam, Isaac and Bishop's family members.

That's when the trouble started because Dam and Isaac had informed attendees that in God's eye everyone was a VIP. So, when the pastors and bishops showed up with their VIP cards in hand and discovered that the common folks were sitting in their seats, they got the ushers involved. The ushers were going to each person, asking if they had a VIP card. If the person didn't have it, they were asked to move.

But the crowd wasn't having it. As Dam was helping Amarrea and his sweet baby girl, Jewel to their seats, he heard one lady hollering at the usher. "I got here early enough to claim this seat. If them 3-piece suit wearing jokers wanted this seat, then they should have gotten here early like I did."

Others could then be heard murmuring and complaining about changing seats. The ushers didn't know what to do. Service was about to start within the next five minutes, but it looked more like a fight was about to break out.

Dam made his way to the stage and grabbed hold of the microphone. "Good evening, I want to thank you all so much for coming out tonight. We will be getting started in a few minutes, so we need everyone to take their seats."

"We're trying," One of the bishops yelled at him. "But these people won't get out of our seats."

The bishop said the word 'people' as if the word was dirty and he might need a bath after using it. Dam couldn't understand how preachers could have so much disdain for the very people God called them to serve in the first place. But he'd seen preachers mistreat God's people. Did they think the scripture, 'touch not my anointed and do my prophet no harm' was only talking about preachers?

"Bishop Thomas promised us VIP seats. Y'all need to run a tighter ship around here. I don't let people come into my church and just take over." The preacher looked as if he was standing in a crowd of homeless people who hadn't bathed in weeks.

"And where is my armor bearer supposed to sit," another one yelled out.

Dam had just about had enough. He pointed toward the bleachers. "We have plenty of seats still available. Anyone who doesn't already have a seat on the field will have to go the bleachers. We thank you so much for your cooperation."

As the preachers headed for the bleachers, one of the preachers said, "God is not the author of confusion."

No, Dam thought, God is not, but Bishop Thomas sure is. Despite all of Bishop's antics with trying to take over and run the show as if the crusade was a ministry he birthed, the rest of the event scheduled for that night proceeded as planned.

The mayor of the city and the governor of the state attended the event and presented a plaque declaring the first day of the crusade to be Isaac Walker Sr. Day. Donovan, Iona, and Isaac stood on the stage as the plaques were presented. The entire Walker family teared up during the presentation. Isaac Walker Sr. was a great man, and it is good that he be honored in this way.

Isaac lifted the plaque heavenward. "This one's for you, Dad."

Praise and worship got the crowd on their feet, but Bishop Thomas tore the house down when he preached a message, titled, Stay Humble. Even with everything they had gone through with Bishop Thomas, Dam and Isaac found themselves jumping out of their seat, high-fiving each other and amening the bishop as he preached his heart out.

When service was over, not many came to the altar that night, but Dam and Isaac still believed the night was a success. "Whoa, did you see how the crowd responded to his message. I don't even want to preach tomorrow after that," Isaac said.

"You better go on and do what God told you to do. Your message is going to speak to the hearts of the people," Dam assured him.

"Do you know what you're going to preach about."

Dam shook his head. "God hasn't given me one single word yet. I've been praying and praying about it. Amarrea says that I'm overthinking this. But hey, since Bishop is going to preach on the third night. I don't have to worry about it until the fourth night of the crusade, right."

Bishop walked over to them and put arms around them as if they were the best of friends. "God is up to something with this crusade. I can feel it. Thank you so much for allowing me to be a part of it."

Dam and Isaac were left speechless, and Bishop walked away. It took a few seconds, but finally, Isaac said, "Is that the same man we've been dealing with?"

"Maybe God has truly gotten hold of him." Dam was amazed at the turnaround. But he had enough faith in God to believe anything was possible.

~~~

Jade was at home watching the broadcast of the crusade. If she didn't know her husband like the back of her hand, she would swear God had gotten hold of him. It was that or...

She wasn't big on discerning spirits like the saints talked about. But she could discern Daniel Thomas' spirit. She picked up the phone and called him. Bishop answered on the first ring. In the past few years, he'd never picked up one of her calls before the third or fourth ring. Sometimes he didn't pick up at all, and just called her back when he had time. The life of a bishop, just busy, busy, busy.

"Hey babe, how are you doing tonight?" Bishop asked.

"I'm doing good. I just watched your sermon, it truly moved me."

"I wish you could have been here with us tonight, Jade. I truly missed having you with me. Do you think you can come out to the crusade this week and labor with us?"

She hesitated a moment, then said, "I just might do that. But look, the reason I'm calling is that I know how you like to through parties for your VIP after conventions. I didn't want to be selfish and not allow you to use the house this week if you wanted to host some of your friends."

"You would do that for me?"

"Look, Daniel, I'm not your enemy. If you need the house, I can stay in your hotel room and let you host your friends."

"Are you sure you wouldn't need to come back to the house for anything?"

"Don't I always leave when you host your VIPs?"

"Okay then. I'll pack up and be at the house in the morning. And Jade…"

"Yes, Daniel?"

"Thank you. I truly have come to realize just how much you mean to me in these weeks that we have been apart."

"I'm sure I will see how much I mean to you before the week is out." She hung up with bishop but immediately placed another call, then began packing a bag so she could go and enjoy room service on the bishop.

~~~

The second night of the crusade was even better than the first. Where they had empty seats in the bleacher section on the first night, there wasn't an empty seat in the place when Isaac stood behind the podium and delivered his message on forgiveness. When Isaac was finished, the altar was flooded by weeping and repented souls.

"All I can say is wow," Dam said to Isaac as they left the crusade for the night. "You got that message straight from the throne room."

Isaac nodded. "Yes, I did. It is time for all of us to learn how to forgive so that we can truly accept the forgiveness that God wants to give to us."

"Amen, brother. Amen."

Amarrea had stayed home with Jewel because their one-month-old baby didn't enjoy sitting still for hours. When Dam got home, he found his wife in bed. "Did you watch the crusade tonight?"

"I sure did, from what I just heard on CNN, the viewership went from one million last night to 4.5 million tonight."

"Are you kidding me?" Dam couldn't believe what he was hearing. God was truly blessing the crusade and allowing their message to get out to a hurting world.

"No, I'm not kidding." Amarrea pulled the cover back. "Come to bed, you look exhausted."

"I will, I just want to see Jewel first." Dam took off his jacket and undid his tie. He then went into the nursery which was next to their bedroom and stared at his sleeping angel. There had been so much stress and pain involved in bringing Jewel into the world. But as he looked at her, sleeping peacefully in her baby bed, Dam knew that he and Amarrea would do it all over again.

Leaning into the bed, his kissed his sweet princess on the cheek. She stirred, flopped her arms a bit and then settled down again. Dam was tempted to wake her so he could have the pleasure of sitting in the rocking chair and rock her to sleep. But his body was aching. He was hesitant to start something he might not be able to finish.

He jumped into the shower, then put on a pair of pajama pants and came to bed. Dam pulled Amarrea into his arms and kissed the back of her neck. "I love holding you like this."

"Yeah, holding me until you fall asleep." Amarrea laughed at him.

"I know I've been falling asleep on you lately. But the body is exhausted. I promise I'll do better once this crusade is over."

Amarrea shook her head. "Bae, I don't think you understand what you and Isaac have started. This crusade will probably last until Jesus returns. Next, you'll be traveling from this town to that."

"You really think so?" Dam yawned.

"I think this is the moment that God has been preparing you for all your life. You better get that sermon ready… don't embarrass us when it's your turn to preach."

"There you go with that mouth of yours." Dam tickled his wife. As Amarrea giggled and squirmed Dam forgot all about how tired he was and held onto his wife as if the world was ending. By morning Dam wished the world had ended, then he wouldn't have to deal with the firestorm that had just rained down on them.

15

"Turn on the news, man. We have got a serious problem this time," Isaac said during his 6 a.m. phone call to Dam.

Dam rubbed his eyes and tried to sit up in bed. "What's going on?"

"Remember that problem we didn't take care of? Well, it has struck again."

"Bishop? But he's been doing so good lately."

"Turn on the TV, Dam. We're done." Isaac sounded despondent.

Dam nudged Amarrea. "Huh? What?" Her eyes were still closed as she tried to respond.

"Hand me the remote, hon."

With her eyes still half closed, Amarrea searched the nightstand for the remote. Finding it, she handed it to Dam then flopped her head back on the pillow.

Dam turned on the television then made his way to a local news channel. A news reporter was standing outside Bishop Thomas' home interviewing First Lady Jade. He said, "I'm sure our viewers would like to know why you turned over this kind of damaging footage of your husband and several other world-renowned pastors?"

Jade didn't miss a beat, she quickly answered, "Because I'm so tired of these holier-than-thou preachers telling us one way to live when they live any kind of way they want. Their actions should be judged by God and man."

"Well you heard it first here on Channel 9," The reporter said. "Now I must caution you, if there are children in the room, you will want to change the channel or get them out of the room. The footage we are about to show you is both graphic and disturbing."

"Did you already see the footage," Dam asked Isaac.

"Man, you are not going to believe this. Jade put cameras in the basement and caught Bishop red-handed. You just need to watch, because I can't even repeat some of the stuff I saw this morning."

"It can't be that bad," Dam said, refusing to believe that Bishop could do anything worse than what he'd already done. But all his hopes were dashed as the footage quickly rolled.

A feast was set up on one of the tables. Ham, Turkey, Mac & cheese. It was like a Thanksgiving meal. Bishop could be seen pouring drinks behind the bar in his basement. The bar was fully stocked with all types of alcohol. Another well-known preacher who was on the speaking circuit and had sold millions of how-to-live-Godly books was behind another table spreading out lines of cocaine. A gospel singer who had been rumored to have AIDs was at the party as well.

When the preacher finished creating the lines of coke, he held up tiny straws and said, "Come and get it."

The men and women at the party snorted and drank and ate to their hearts were content. They laid mattresses on the floor and then they began taking off their clothes.

"I am not seeing what I am seeing?" Dam said.

By this time, Amarrea had rolled over and was watching the television with him. "Oh, you're seeing it alright. I'm just thankful that they have shaded out some of the body parts on those naked, shameful people."

"They are straight clowning," Isaac said.

Unfortunately, they hadn't seen the worst of it. Dam could hardly believe that the footage had only been going for a few minutes. The news station had edited the footage in such a way that they were showing clips of all the madness that was going on. Finally reaching its climax as the viewers witnessed these preachers, gospel singers, and so-called armor bearers having sex with each other. Men and women were having sex, women were with women, and the men were with men. It was an abomination on full display.

Finally, the reporter who was standing in front of Bishop's house came back into view, and the footage was cut. He said, "Sadly enough, some of the men and women who were attending that party and participating in drug, alcohol use and even the orgy are the same people who preach against these acts each week behind their pulpits. Jade Thomas has done the world a great service by exposing these hypocrites."

The camera panned back to the newsroom. And the reporter behind the desk asked, "Isn't Bishop Thomas one of the preachers hosting this crusade that's getting millions of viewers and filling up our football stadium?"

"No! Don't talk about the crusade," Amarrea shouted at the television.

Screaming at the TV didn't change the situation. The reporters not only discussed the crusade, but they also mentioned Isaac and Dam and wondered aloud if either one of them had been at that party.

Thankfully, the reporter on the scene stated, "I can confirm that neither Isaac Walker Jr. or Dam Shepherd was at that party."

Jade grabbed the microphone from the reporter as she shouted into it. "The Bishop is good at hiding his secrets. Only a select few knew the truth about this man. But now the world knows."

~~~

"What are we going to do about this? My phone has been ringing off the hook with reporters wanting to interview me about Bishop. And church members calling asking if I would just start my own church so they could leave Call of God," Dam told Isaac as they met at Isaac's church later that afternoon.

"I turned my phone off. I can't deal with any more distractions before we head to the crusade tonight," Isaac said.

"Do you think we should do the crusade tonight. I was thinking that we should maybe cancel it. At least for tonight."

Isaac shook his head. "We cannot let Bishop destroy what God is building."

"But hasn't he already destroyed it. I've seen the comments all over social media saying that preachers are all alike and that they can't trust any of us. People are proudly declaring that they live in sin and that they will never hide behind some false God."

"All the more reason why we can't quit. You and I have to show the world that God does exist and that there are real consequences for sin. But more than that… we have to show them that there is a God who wants to forgive them and love on them."

"Did you forget that Bishop is supposed to preach tonight?"

"I wish he would," Isaac's fist clenched as if he was spooling for a fight.

"Then who is going to preach," Dam asked.

Isaac pointed at him. "You're up bro. It's time for the world to hear what you've got to say."

"But God hasn't given me a word yet. I've been praying about it, but… nothing."

"Then might I suggest you get out of here and go home so you can prepare. Because one of us has to bring the word tonight. And I already preached last night."

Dam and Isaac clasped hands. "Alright, let me get out of here. You're right, Isaac. It's too late for us to turn back now."

"I'll call Bishop and let him know that he's done."

"Good luck with that," Dam said as he headed home.

Amarrea greeted him at the door with Jewel in her arms. Jewel took one look at him and smiled so bright that he had to hold her. "Sweet, sweet Jewel. Please stay just as innocent as you are now. Don't let this sinful world change you."

"Oh, she won't. Because I'm going to spank that bottom every time she gets out of line."

"How could you want to spank a cute little baby, like this?" Dam played with his baby girl. He blew kisses and rubbed noses, then he realized that he wouldn't be able to stay home if he was going to put a sermon together.

He handed Jewel back to Amarrea, went into his home office, grabbed his Bible, a notepad and left the house. Dam drove down to the stadium. He took his seat on the grand stage and looked out at the chairs and bleacher seats. There was space for fifty thousand people. The place was full last night, he wondered if anyone would even bother to show up tonight.

Opening his Bible Dam turned to 2 Timothy, chapter 4. As he began reading his heart was filled with sorrow…

I charge thee therefore before God, and the Lord Jesus Christ, who shall judge the quick and the dead at his appearing and his kingdom; Preach the word; be instant in season, out of season; reprove, rebuke, exhort with all longsuffering and doctrine.

For the time will come when they will not endure sound doctrine; but after their own lusts shall they heap to themselves teachers, having itching ears; And they shall turn away their ears from the truth, and shall be turned unto fables.

With everything in him, Dam knew that they were now living in the days when people did not want to hear the truth, but only wanted to hear messages that pleased the flesh. He had never been that kind of preacher and sure wasn't about to become it tonight. Dam bowed his head to pray. But then he heard a noise that caused him to look toward the field. Someone was walking toward the stage. Dam hoped it was not a reporter looking for another scoop. He didn't have time for all the drama that surrounded his boss. He stood up and walked over to the podium. Turning the microphone on, Dam spoke into it. "Service doesn't begin until seven tonight. And we won't be seating anyone until five."

The man kept walking towards him, Dam held the microphone to his mouth again, "Did you hear me. There's nothing going on here until later tonight."

As Dam put the microphone down, the man was now close enough for Dam to see who he was. It was Bishop.

"Why do you think I'm here, Dam? I know service doesn't begin yet. I need a place where I can be alone so I can think. I can't write my sermon in peace with the firestorm my lovely wife created."

"Do you really think your wife created your problems? Or was it you and that party you and several other men and women of God participated in?"

"Jade tricked me. She set those cameras up in our basement and then lured me over there. I never should have married that woman. I

113

knew she was no good when she smiled in my dying wife's face, all the while putting her hooks in me."

Dam had never hated anyone in his life, and as Bishop Thomas stood in front of him, unrepented for the things he had done, Dam tried to remind himself that it was the sin he hated and not the person. "Is this for real, or have you lost your mind?"

"Is what for real?" Bishop looked as if he didn't understand what was bothering Dam.

"Do you really think you're going to preach tonight?"

"Why wouldn't I? I'm on the schedule, and this gives me the perfect opportunity to address those doctored up tapes the fake news media put out on me this morning."

"It didn't look like fake news to me."

With frustration etched on his face, Bishop waved his hand in the air as if dismissing Dam. "I don't have to explain nothing to you. I need to pray and work on my sermon so just leave me alone."

Standing firm, Dam said, "I don't think you understand me. You are no longer a part of this crusade. Isaac and I made the decision earlier today, and he left you a message stating that fact. I will be preaching tonight."

"You!" Bishop balked at the thought. "You are too wet behind the ears to handle a crowd of this size. You'll freeze like a deer caught in headlights."

"Stay humble, Bishop." Dam couldn't help himself. He smirked as he recited the title of the sermon the bishop gave the other day.

"Why I ought to," Bishop raise a fisted hand as if he wanted to strike Dam.

"Don't come for me, Bishop. I come from a long line of men who would kill you for raising a hand to them." Dam set his feet and got his hands ready to fight if need be. "I don't believe in violence, but I will defend myself if I have to."

"You threatening me, boy? I guess this means you don't need your job anymore?"

Dam was losing his patience for this man. "I wouldn't work for you if I was getting paid a million dollars a year. My wife and I will no longer be attending your church either."

"Don't start a fight that you can't win, Dam. I will destroy you if you try to leave my church or take my members."

Dam would have laughed if the situation wasn't so sad. "Bishop, can't you see that you've already destroyed yourself. You need to repent before it's too late. I believe you started out wanting to please God, but you got lost somewhere. Ask God to help you find yourself again."

"I don't need no advice from you. Get out of here and let me get ready for my sermon."

At that moment Isaac stepped onto the stage with them. He told Bishop, "We will have you arrested if you get on this stage tonight. Do you hear me, Bishop? If you think you have trouble now, try adding a trespassing charge to your list."

"Do you know who I am!" Bishop exploded. "I am one of the most renowned bishops in the United States. I have traveled the world doing God's work, and the two of you think you can bully me?"

"We're not trying to bully you. We just don't want any more drama while we're trying to do God's business," Dam told him. "Not even you, Bishop Thomas, as world-renowned as you might be can stand in the way of God's work. We won't allow it."

"You're fired!" Bishop brushed past Dam and Isaac. "Y'all don't know who you're dealing with, but I'm gon' show you."

16

Bishop Thomas spent the rest of the afternoon calling television networks and informing them that he would not be speaking tonight. He encouraged each network to pull the plug on the program. The problem though, was that the networks received so much positive feedback and growth in viewership that they couldn't ignore the crusade now.

When Bishop was informed of that very fact, he became angry and blurted out, "Then cancel my program from your network. Maybe you don't need the money that I pay your network each and every month."

Bishop was then told, "In light of recent developments, we were actually planning to contact you about your contract with our network. But we thank you for agreeing to discontinue your program."

"Wait a minute. I didn't agree to any such thing." Bishop thought if he threatened to cancel his program they would think twice about covering the crusade. He never thought they would want him to leave, not after all the years he's partnered with the Christian network.

"We're sorry Bishop, but we think it is for the best. We will be praying for you," was the last words spoken as they hung up the phone.

Bishop then called his attorney. "Listen here Bill, I have a problem I need you to help me solve."

"I saw. How you get caught up like that?"

"I'm not talking about that doctored up recording my wife made in order to use for her divorce attorney. You know me better than that. You know I am a true man of God."

Bill didn't confirm or deny, he just said, "What can I do for you, Bishop?"

"Them jokers I allowed to partner with me on this crusade are now trying to shut me out. I need to get an injunction to shut this crusade down."

"What would be the reason for the injunction?"

"Dam and Isaac are cheats. They want to keep all that offering money to themselves, even though I'm the reason we have such a huge crowd in the first place."

"Did the three of you have a contract?" Bill asked.

"A handshake should be good enough. Now get that injunction."

~~~

As Dam stood behind the pulpit trying to get a feel for how it would be to preach to a massive crowd, that is, if the people showed up, after how Bishop got their names ran through the mud right along with his. Looking out at the sea of chairs and the bleachers that would most likely be full later tonight, he wondered if the bishop was right… was he too wet behind the ears? Or had God created him for such a time as this? Could he truly stand behind the pulpit and deliver God's message to all these people without wavering; would these people want to hear what he had to say?

As he looked to heaven wondering what God was thinking to give him this overwhelming assignment at such a young age, he caught a glimpse of something going on up there. Dam closed his eyes and shook his head before he looked to the skies again.

An angel opened the door of heaven. Dam wondered if he was once again about to be translated to the heavenly as Apostle Paul had been. But then something that looked like a slide was rolled out until it reached the earth. Then he saw legions of angels marching their way toward the earth with swords drawn as they sang a song that Dam could not understand the words too. "What is going on?" Dam asked.

Then in the next moment Dam's eyes were drawn to the deepest, darkest part of the earth as an eery crawling feeling crept up his spine. There, he saw demons and imps slithering and sliming their way out of hell. "Where are they going, Lord?"

Preach the word.

"Yes Lord, I hear you." Dam was no longer concerned about his inadequacy. The Lord was on his side, and he was on the Lord's side. They would get through whatever this was. All he had to do was preach the word and let God handle the rest. Just like his daughter only had to lay in Amarrea's stomach and be pushed out of her body. And with that thought, Dam's sermon began to take form.

~~~

"Whatcha doing?" Marissa asked Isaac as she found him sitting on the back patio just staring up at the sky.

" Just thinking?" Isaac answered.

"Do you want to be alone? Because I can always find something to do in the house."

"No bae." He patted the cushion next to him. "Come and sit with me."

Cozying up next to her husband, Marissa said, "I hope you're not letting that awful Bishop Thomas get to you. That man is not going to destroy your father's legacy. I can promise you that."

Isaac shook his head. He took Marissa's hand in his. "I need you to trust your man on this. I know I sent you through as I tried to come to terms with my parents leaving me so soon. But I'm done with that."

"I know you are. But this crusade means so much to you. I just wanted to make sure that you weren't back here mopping around like everything has been ruined. Because God got this," Marissa declared.

Smiling at his wife, Isaac said, "Let me share with you something that God revealed to me. Do you remember when you asked me to go with you to Amarrea and Dam's wedding?"

"Ah-huh. I remember that you didn't want to go, I had to drag you kicking and screaming. But once you were there, you acted like a gentleman throughout the entire ceremony."

Lifting a finger, Isaac said, "Yes, I did act like that. But I believe that day was one of God's divine appointments in my life. Who would have known that I had married a woman who was best friends with the woman who was marrying a man like Dam Shepherd? God connected me and that brother."

"Do you know how happy it makes me that you and Dam became friends? It makes it that much easier for Amarrea and I to hang out together."

"But it's not just about the friendship... do you remember the story of King David in the Bible and the temple he wanted to build for God?"

Marissa nodded.

"King David had been a warrior and had killed many men. Even though God loved him and David blessed him during his lifetime. He told him that he could not build the temple because there was too much blood on his hands. After King David's death, God allowed his son to build the temple.

"I believe that God is doing the same thing right now with Dam and me at this crusade. Yeah, we messed up by allowing Bishop Thomas to join in with us. But that's not going to stop God. Because I truly believe that He is allowing Isaac Walker Sr.'s son to take this crusade to places my father would not have been able to take it due to his previous lifestyle."

"As a girl who came from the streets and saw so much of the harm that men do to each other, I can understand what you're saying."

Isaac clasped his hands as he said, "So, now you understand why nothing Bishop Thomas can do will cause me one moment of doubt. I'm looking forward to finishing what my father started, and I count it an honor that God saw fit for Dam and me to finish the job that Keith and my dad could not."

~~~

Word got around that the crusade was still going on. Most of the people thought for sure it would be canceled after the most well-known member of the crusade had been uncovered, so to speak. But now curiosity was building. People wanted to know who would preach tonight. Would Bishop Thomas dare to show his face? Would he have the nerve to sit on the stage with the rest of the preachers?

Not only were the people excited to get down to the crusade, but local, and national newscasters were flying in with their camera crews. They were planning to cover this crusade like it was a hurricane and each and every network needed to be there. Some of the top anchors from CNN, MSNBC and FOX news had stationed themselves just outside the crusade and were setting up to broadcast live. No one wanted to be the network who missed the opportunity to show the world the demise of Christianity. Because surely, no one would ever believe a word these people said again… because if the preachers and leaders in the faith community couldn't live right, how in the world did they expect anyone else to do it. Today, they would show the world that the Bible was an outdated book and needed to be banned and taken out of stores.

~~~

Iona, her husband Johnny and their kids, met up with Donovan, his wife Dianne and their children. They were dressed and ready to go to the crusade. "I've got a feeling that we need to get down their early, or we just might be fighting for a seat," Dianne said.

But Donovan disagreed. "With all that has happened this week, we don't want to cause any more problems. If our seats are gone, we'll just sit in the bleachers."

"Speak for yourself," Iona quipped. "If my seat is gone, I'm fighting."

"Johnny, man, please do something with your wife." Donovan just shook his head.

Johnny put his arms around his wife. "After all these years, I've learned to just love her and get out of the way."

The group laughed as they all headed out the door.

~~~

Jade was furious when she arrived back at her house and discovered that the locks had been changed. Banging on the door, she demanded, "Let me in. This is my house too."

121

No one responded. Jade went around the back. She picked up one of the bricks from the beautifully designed garden and tried to break the window with it. The window didn't even crack. "I know you're in there, Daniel. You better let me in this house right now. I'm not playing with you."

"The bishop isn't there," the little boy from the house next door told Jade as he stood on the back porch."

"Where is he?" Jade harshly questioned the little boy. Then she calmed herself down. "I'm sorry. Ms. Jade didn't mean to yell at you."

"You don't have to apologize to us," the boy's mother said as she joined her son on the back porch. "We are praying for you, Jade. With all that so-called preacher has put you through, you'd think he'd just give you that house. He's got some nerve."

"Oh, I plan to get this house and much more, because I'm divorcing him. I'm done with him."

"Good for you."

As Jade looked at the time, she realized that she knew exactly where Daniel had taken himself. She waved at the woman. "I'll see you later, I need to go get my keys."

~~~

The Shepherd family was in the house. Angel, Demetrius and all their children from DeMarcus, Dee, Dontae to Dodi. There was no way any of them were going to miss this night. From the time Dam was born, they all knew he was special. God had a work for this young man to do and they believed the work would truly begin tonight.

DeMarcus, the former football player, leaned forward and said to his parents, "I used to play on fields this big, and I still don't remember seeing this many people at one of our games."

"They've added the chairs on the football field, so I guess there are more people here than would attend the game," Demetrius said.

"And our son is about to preach to all of these people." Angel looked around in awe of what she saw.

"I can't believe that my little brother is like some big-time preacher." Dee just shook his head. "I told him that he was my hero. And I meant that."

Angel might have been in awe at all the people she saw in this place on the night that her son was about to preach. But she had no problem believing that this thing had come to pass. It had been prophesied even while he was in her stomach.

She still remembered that day just like it was yesterday. Angel and Demetrius were at odds over her pregnancy. So, she had driven to an abortion clinic with plans to end her pregnancy…

Angel pulled into the lot and checked the time. Her appointment was scheduled for 9 a.m. She was twenty minutes early, so she sat in her car and took a few deep breaths. Taking the key out of the ignition, Angel looked out at the street, and that's when she noticed the people holding picket signs.

One sign said, 'Don't Kill Your Baby… Every Life Matters. Then another sign had on it, 'Jeremiah 1:5'.

The scripture was not written on that poster, but it didn't have to be. It was the same scripture her father used to read to her when she was a child: Before I formed you in the womb I knew you; Before you were born I sanctified you.

As the words of Jeremiah shocked her system, Angel once again realized why she thought of abortion as murder. Because if God knew a child and could sanctify him or her before they were even born, then the so-called fetus had to be a living thing. Angel was undone. All she had done was love a man who loved her and their family more than anything else. But life had dealt them a blow, and now she didn't know what to do, didn't know how to choose right rather than wrong.

Tears were blurring her eyes as the woman who'd been holding the 'Every Life Matters' poster knocked on her door. Angel wiped her face and rolled down the window.

The woman asked, "Would you like to talk to someone?"

Angel nodded as she unlocked the door and allowed the woman to get in the car.

The woman extended her hand. "I'm Patricia Miller-Harding. You don't have to cry anymore because God sent me here for you."

"Why would God send you to me?"

"You don't believe me?" Patricia put a gentle hand on Angel's shoulder as she said, "I know everything about you, Angel."

"How do you know my name?"

"God has given me a glimpse into your life... I know that your upbringing was all about the Lord and growing closer to Him. Until your parent's divorce, you had even planned to go into the ministry yourself. But then you ran away, moved in with a street-wise guy, and when he tossed you out, instead of humbling yourself and going back to your parents, who had re-married, you started stripping, and then you fell in love with another criminal. You married him, now he has you here, about to kill one of God's soldiers."

"Who are you?" were the only words Angel could form. She was stunned that this woman could read her. What was going on?

"I'm a friend, sent by the Lord with a message for you."

"What's the message," Angel asked, still feeling a little devastated by the way she'd just been read.

Patricia looked directly into Angel's eyes and held onto her hands as she said, "Thus says the Lord, you were born to serve God, you chose not to... but this baby you are carrying will not be swayed by the enemy. He will do great and mighty things for the Lord."

Exhaling, Angel put her hand into Demetrius' hand and squeezed it while she thanked God for sending that woman to her when she needed her most. Her family had stayed together, and now her son, the one sent from God was doing just what had been prophesied of him.

17

As praise and worship ended, Dam stood behind the podium, he wasn't distracted by the large crowd that had gathered nor was he distracted by the spiritual battle God kept giving him glimpses of. It was his turn to preach, and he was going to do what God called him to do.

"Before I begin, I want to thank all of you for coming out tonight. I'm not sure if you're here because you want to hear the word or if you thought there might be some more foolishness going on, but either way, thank you. Because now I get to deliver to you, what God has dropped in my spirit." He smiled out toward the crowd of people, then said, "Turn with me to the book of Isaiah, chapter 13. I'm going to begin reading at verse six.

"Howl ye; for the day of the Lord is at hand; it shall come as a destruction from the Almighty. Therefore shall all hands be faint, and every man's heart shall melt:

And they shall be afraid: pangs and sorrows shall take hold of them; they shall be in pain as a woman that travaileth: they shall be amazed one at another; their faces shall be as flames. Behold, the day of the Lord cometh, cruel both with wrath and fierce anger, to lay the land desolate: and he shall destroy the sinners thereof out of it.

For the stars of heaven and the constellations thereof shall not give their light: the sun shall be darkened in his going forth, and the moon shall not cause her light to shine. And I will punish the world for their evil, and the wicked for their iniquity; and I will cause the arrogancy of the proud to cease, and will lay low the haughtiness of the terrible.

When Dam closed the Bible and looked out at the crowd, he said, "My wife and I just had a baby, so I understand very well what these scriptures are talking about as it relates to a woman travailing. Bringing a child forth is not a pretty thing. It involves pain and sometimes sorrows as you go through the process. But then we rejoiced as a new life was brought into the world.

"And if you think about it, living a life full of sin is like a woman suffering to bring forth a new life. You go through highs and lows. One moment there's no pain, and things seem fine, so you keep living your life, doing whatever feels good. But the next moment the pain which is the consequences of sin hit you and turn your life upside down. That's when you begin to reach out for something, anything you can hold onto to help ease the pain. For my wife, it was my hand. She almost broke my hand off when those labor pains hit her." Dam flicked his hand as if it was still in pain, the crowd laughed, and he laughed right along with them.

When the laughter stopped, Dam then asked the crowd, "What about you? What do you grab hold of when the pains of life are more than you can bear? Have you ever thought about giving my friend, Jesus a try?"

"I know that today's Christians have given my Lord and Savior a bad name. Christians don't tell the truth anymore. You can't trust that they will do what they committed to. Christians sin as if there is no God. But my God won't be mocked. As it says in the scriptures I just read, God will punish the world for their evil and the wicked for their iniquities."

Bishop Thomas felt as if he was in a fishbowl and all eyes were on him. He wanted to get up and walk out of the stadium. But he was afraid that he would draw even more attention to himself. And the way Dam was preaching and calling out the sins of Christians, Bishop knew for sure those reporters who were now at the back of the stadium would stop him. They would then ask him all sorts of questions that he had no answers for.

And with the way Dam was preaching, Bishop wondered who in this stadium could give an answer for the way in which they had lived their lives. When he started off in the ministry, Bishop only wanted to please God. But then the church members kept telling him how anointed he was. He was told that he needed to do radio... then he needed to do television... then he needed to get on the speaking circuit.

Once he'd done everything the people told him he needed to do, there didn't seem to be any part of God left in his ministry. And that's when it became easy to succumb to all the lustful things this world had to offer. If he could turn back the hands of time, he would do it differently. But things had spiraled too far out of control, and Bishop didn't know how to make what was wrong right again.

Dam was saying, "But there is hope. The God I serve is a forgiving God. He wants to forgive you and help you walk upright before Him.

Will you repent and turn away from sin? Will you let God have total control of your life?"

Dam then looked directly into the camera and said, "You may be sitting on your sofa, watching this broadcast from home. You think I'm just talking to the people in this stadium." He pointed at the camera, toward that person at home that God was trying to reach. "But God's word is for you also. You can repent right where you sit."

Tears flowed down Dam's eyes as he turned back to the people in the stadium. "God's free gift of salvation is for you also. Won't you come down here? Repent and give God your whole heart. I promise that He won't abuse or misuse you as the world has done so many times."

"Come on, my friends, if you are ready to truly live for God and forsake this sinful world, then come down here and stand with me."

One by one, two by two, then three by three the people started to get out of their seats and head down to the area just below the stage. Dam couldn't see the angels anymore, but he knew they were out there fighting the good fight of faith against the demonic forces that tried to hold anyone who belonged to God in their seats.

God would get the glory this night and Dam would stand there as long as it took. He would wait until everyone who wanted to give their lives to God was standing before him.

Isaac got out of his seat and came to stand next to Dam. He turned his microphone back on as he yelled out to the crowd, "There's still room at the cross. Don't let it be said, too late… too late." And just like that, the altar was flooded.

Tears of regret and pain streamed down the faces of thousands of men and women who made their way to the altar. There were so many at the altar that the chairs on the football field had to be removed.

Dam felt the power of the Holy Spirit moving within him like never before. This is it… this is truly the mission God had for him.

He would not leave this stage until every soul in need of salvation got what they came to the altar for. "Can't you feel it, my friends? God is here with us. He wants to save you from your sins. He wants to clean your heart and make you brand new."

Agonizing moaning and groaning came from the people. Some stood, some got down on bended knees, and some laid prostrate on the ground. "Help us, Lord!", "Make me new.", "I'm so tired of how I've been living, Lord.", "I want to live for God.", were some of the words Dam heard the people say as the cried out to God.

They were ready. As he looked out at the sea of repented souls, he said, "Just lift your hands and repeat after me, Lord, I am so sorry for the way I've lived my life. I'm tired of all the pain and the strife. Thank you for sending Your son Jesus to save me from my sins; to cleanse me and make me new, just as a baby is born of the flesh. I thank You that I can accept Your free gift of salvation and be born again of the spirit."

Without hesitation, the people lifted their hands and repeated after Dam. The people who stood at the altar were guilty of every sin imaginable... abortion, murder, adultery, fornication, homosexuality, lying, stealing, backbiting and so much more. All sin was equal in God's eyes, and all of their sins were instantly washed away, cleansed in the blood of Jesus.

"Do you see what's happening?" Isaac asked Dam as they stood before the people.

Dam nodded. "They have truly repented. And their sins have been washed away."

Tears of joy were now being shed by all who had come to the altar. But sadly, there were still some who remained in their seats and watched the flow of the Holy Spirit like spectators. Dam wished he could get those people out of their seats so they could partake in this feeling of great joy that the others were feeling. But God would not take their free will. Therefore, they were free to reject this free gift of salvation and continue to live a life full of sin.

When the crusade was over, Dam and Isaac both sat down on opposite sides of the field for interviews with numerous networks. But just as the interviewer began the questions something miraculous occurred. Dam and Isaac disappeared.

But it wasn't just Dam and Isaac who disappeared, some of the reporters disappeared, and many of the people who had been in attendance and had come down to the altar disappeared as well.

"What is going on here?" One of the reporters shouted as he looked around the field and saw clothes and shoes lining the field but nobody was in those clothes. His cameraman had been right in front of him, but now his clothes were on the ground, and the camera was also. "Where did everybody go?"

Great moaning was heard by the people who had been left behind as they held onto the clothes their loved ones had been wearing. "Mama, come back!" One young man screamed.

"Hon, no, don't leave me like this," an old man cried out while holding the dress that had belonged to his wife of sixty years.

When Bishop Thomas noticed that neither Dam or Isaac was around to settle the crowd down. He rushed to the stage and grabbed the microphone. "Calm down everyone. Something very wrong has occurred, but we will get to the bottom of this."

He was holding a blouse and a pair of pants in his hands. He lifted them so everyone could see, "I was just standing down there talking to my wife. She came to me with tears in her eyes and apologized to me for doctoring those videos that she gave to the

131

news station. She asked me to forgive her and I did just that. But she disappeared before I could bring her up here to clear everything up."

The reporter who'd just lost his cameraman. Grabbed hold of the camera and joined Bishop Thomas on the stage. "Are you saying that the video footage we watched of your illicit orgy was doctored?"

"That is exactly what I'm saying." Bishop puffed out his chest.

"So, that wasn't you we saw on that footage, is that what you're saying?"

"Of course, it wasn't me. I am a man of God. I have been dedicated to God since I was a youth. The good Lord has blessed me and my ministry. Would I have been able to put on such a crusade that caused so many to give their lives to God if I was such a sinful man?"

The reporter faced the camera he was holding and said, "You heard it here first. Bishop Thomas says that his wife doctored those tapes we viewed of him and other pastors partying like rock stars. And since his wife is now missing, we'll have to do a little more investigating to get to the bottom of this."

People began rushing the stage, asking, "Where did they go? Have they been raptured? Is it too late for me to repent? I want to repent for my sins, please let me repent now."

But it indeed was too late.

Epilogue

While the earth experienced the great tribulation, a celebration was going on in a new land that had been created for those who loved God and did His will… for those who endured until the end.

Isaac Walker Senior and Nina Walker walked over to the newest member of the Walker family. Isaac took Junior in his arms and said, "I've been waiting to hold you since the day you were born. Nice to meet you little one."

"He's so handsome," Nina said as she smiled at the little one.

Dam held onto Amarrea's hand. "We did it, hon. We made it in the rapture." Their eyes filled with awe and amazement as they look around at the sea of people standing around in white garments. Don Shepherd put his hands out for Jewel to come to him. She left her mother's hip and clung to Don. "It is so nice to finally see you, my beautiful little one."

Everyone in this new land had been washed in the blood of the Lamb, they were new creations in Christ. Even as the Shepherd family, the Walker family and many other families reunited in this wondrous new land, they each knew that life would never be the same again. And they were grateful that they had not been left behind but would forever be able to rejoice in the joy of the Lord.

The servant of God, Obadiah Damerae Shepherd, was taken to a room with a brilliant white floor, it looked as if he was stepping on clouds. There must have been some kind of trick mirror in the room because it looked as if thousands of sixty-inch television sets were floating throughout the room.

A door opened on the other side of the room, and a man in a purple garment with the crown of a king on his head walked into the room. He held open his hands as if to give Dam a hug. But that's when Dam noticed the holes in the man's hands. He fell to his knees and bowed his head, "My Lord."

"Yes Obadiah, great servant of God, it is I. But today, I am not just Lord, but also a friend that sticks closer than a brother. And I wanted to greet you and let you see how important it was that you completed the mission we had for you."

Dam was at the point of hyperventilating. "So, I did hear You correctly. I was on the right path?" It came out like a question because with all that Dam went through, there were many times that he questioned whether he'd heard the Lord or if he had just followed after what felt right at the time.

The Lord erupted in laughter. His eyes were bright and filled with love for Dam that was clearly evident. "I do understand why you questioned working for a man like Daniel Thomas. But, we needed you with him so the crusade would be televised."

"Thank You for telling me that. I thought I'd missed it when things started to go bad with Bishop Thomas."

Jesus shook His head. "You didn't miss it. You were always in the will of God. This is the reason you had to be born. We needed a man with the heart of God to lead the last day souls back home to Me."

"I knew I was meant to be in ministry. But in truth, to truly be effective, I would have thought my ministry would need to last for many years. I thought that Isaac and I would have to travel the world to convert the lost."

"Your ways, are not my way," was all the Lord said to that. Then He pointed to seats that were like the recliners found in many theater rooms. "Have a seat, Obadiah. Let me show you what your ministry accomplished tonight."

Dam did as he was instructed. Once he was seated, the flashing lights of the televisions, that weren't actually televisions but more like gigantic screens, came alive. One of the screens moved forward, Dam could see a family sitting in their living room watching him preach the message he delivered at the crusade. When he looked toward the television, pointed at the camera and said, "You may be sitting on your sofa, watching this broadcast from home. You think I'm just talking to the people in this stadium. But God's word is for you also. You can repent right where you sit."

At that moment three of the family members stood up in front of the television. They lifted their hands when Dam asked the people in the stadium to lift their hands and they repeated the sinner's prayer with the others in the stadium. There was only one person in that home who did not receive Jesus into his heart.

That screen moved back, as another came forward. The Lord then showed him a church where the members had gathered to watch the crusade. Hundreds of those members went down to the altar. The same occurred at a sports bar where the crusade was televised… and again, and again in homes all across the country.

Dam turned to Jesus, his eyes full of unshed tears and joy. "All those people accepted You into their hearts because of the crusade?"

Jesus nodded. "You and Isaac did a mighty work, and I will reward both of you in this new life and forever more."

It seemed as if Dam couldn't stop smiling. He was overjoyed that God had found him worthy for this end time ministry. But then he thought of the many people he saw at the stadium and on the screen who had not accepted Christ during the crusade. "What of the people who were left behind, Lord? Is their hope for them?"

With sadness in His eyes, Jesus told him, "They chose the life they wanted, Obadiah. We have left them to men like Daniel Thomas, who will lead them further into paths of unrighteousness.

"But there is one who has been left on earth. When he realizes that he missed the mark, he will do everything it takes to come back to Me, and he will bring others with him. But the rest will go to a place that was designed for Satan and his followers. And there shall be weeping and gnashing of teeth."

"But…" Dam wanted to help those people if he could.

"This is not for you to concern yourself with. You have finished your assignment, now it is time to rest."

And may the Lord be praised!

The end of Book VI

Don't forget to join my mailing list:
http://vanessamiller.com/events/join-mailing-list/
Join me on Facebook: https://www.facebook.com/groups/
77899021863/
Join me on Twitter: https://www.twitter.com/vanessamiller01

Family Business Series

Family Business I

Family Business II - Sword of Division

Family Business III - Love And Honor

Family Business IV - The Children

Family Business V - The Atonement

Family Business VI - Servant of God

About the Author

Vanessa Miller is a best-selling author, playwright, and motivational speaker. She started writing as a child, spending countless hours either reading or writing poetry, short stories, stage plays and novels. Vanessa's creative endeavors took on new meaning in1994 when she became a Christian. Since then, her writing has been centered on themes of redemption, often focusing on characters facing multi-dimensional struggles.

Vanessa's novels have received rave reviews, with several appearing on *Essence Magazine's* Bestseller's List. Miller's work has receiving numerous awards, including "Best Christian Fiction Mahogany Award" and the "Red Rose Award for Excellence in Christian Fiction." Miller graduated from Capital University with a degree in Organizational Communication. She is an ordained minister in her church, explaining, "God has called me to minister to readers and to help them rediscover their place with the Lord."

She has worked with numerous publishers: Urban Christian, Kimani Romance, Abingdon Press and Whitaker House. She is currently indy published through Praise Unlimited enterprises and working on the Family Business Series.

In 2016, Vanessa launched the Christian Book Lover's Retreat in an effort to bring readers and authors of Christian fiction together in an environment that's all about Faith, Fun & Fellowship. To learn more about Vanessa, please visit her website: www.vanessamiller.com. If you would like to know more about the Christian Book Lover's Retreat that is currently held in Charlotte, NC during the last week in October you can visit: http:// www.christianbookloversretreat.com/index.html

Don't forget to join my mailing list:
http://vanessamiller.com/events/join-mailing-list/
Join me on Facebook: https://www.facebook.com/groups/
77899021863/
Join me on Twitter: https://www.twitter.com/vanessamiller01

CPSIA information can be obtained
at www.ICGtesting.com
Printed in the USA
LVHW032107260223
740458LV00003B/674

9 781724 039699